Deptford Literature Festival 2025 Anthology

Featuring work from Spread the Word's 30th Anniversary and Borough of Literature commissioning programmes

Published by Spread the Word

All rights reserved

Copyright in each individual work in this anthology lies with the authors of those works.

The rights of each of the contributors to be identified as authors of their respective works in this anthology have been asserted by them in accordance with section 77 of the Copyright, Designs and Patents Act 1988.

This book is in copyright. Subject to statutory exception and to provisions of relevant collective licensing agreements, no reproduction of any part may take place without the written permission of Spread the Word.

First edition published 2025
ISBN: 978-1-9998254-9-2

Contents

Introduction — 1

30th Anniversary Commissions

Emerging Writer Commissions

Theories of Change, Giselle Cory — 5
Last Orders, Eliezer Gore — 16
To Ears and Tongues, Naomi Walsh — 25

Deaf and Disabled Writer Commissions

Accepting Dirt as Tenderness, Oli Isaac — 39
To my Great Aunty Beryl who didn't speak at first, Ellie Spirrett — 55
Flare: the muted outline of a body in bed as a camera flash overtakes the scene, Jamila Prowse — 61

Borough of Literature Commissions

Sauce, Sprinkles and A Flake Please Boss, Tutku Barbaros — 79
208 from Lewisham Station to Orpington, Perry Hall Road, Amii Griffith — 86
Ode to a Bordertown, Amii Griffith — 88
Musings, Erica Hesketh — 90
Reading A Room of One's Own *on park benches*, Erica Hesketh — 92
Crofton Books, Fathima Zahra — 94
On the 172 and back, Fathima Zahra — 95

About the Contributors — 97

Thanks — 100

Introduction

In 2025 Spread the Word celebrates its 30th anniversary. Set up by Booker Prize-winning author Bernardine Evaristo and Ruth Borthwick, Spread the Word has become London's literature development agency; supporting writers and growing literature audiences across the capital.

It felt fitting to mark this birthday year by focussing on what is central to our work: developing writers from underrepresented backgrounds. From this notion came a series of commissioning strands, supporting ten writers from such backgrounds to create new work.

Our 30th Anniversary commissioning programmes focussed specifically on supporting emerging writers (defined as unagented and unpublished), and D/deaf and/or disabled writers. The former selected by Olumide Popoola and Joelle Taylor; the latter selected by Ayesha Chouglay and Joe Rizzo Naudi. We commissioned three writers for each of these programmes and every writer was supported by a mentor throughout the process; developing their craft as they created new work.

These commissions range from spoken word to lyrical essay; magical realism to poetic image alt-text. All of these pieces capture the excitement of reading captivating work from new writers; something this organisation has championed now for three decades.

***

As well as looking to our past, Spread the Word is looking forwards to the future of literature in London. At Deptford Literature Festival in 2024 we launched our Lewisham Borough of Literature campaign: a programme of work supporting our intention to designate our home of Lewisham as the UK's first Borough of Literature.

A year on, we have appointed an advisory board and are in the midst of consultations with the local community to shape our future plans for the programme. The voices of local writers however are central to this project. Therefore, to mark this new and ambitious step in Spread the Word's history, we commissioned four local writers on the theme of 'to all the places I have read'. Through poetry and prose, you'll be taken on a journey exploring home, community, gentrification, and how we create spaces for art and imagination: from travelling on the 208 bus route and an ice cream van to reading on park benches in Blythe Hill and Mayow Park.

***

All in all, six of the commissions are from writers based in Lewisham, and nine are from writers based in South East London; showing the absolute wealth of talent on our doorstep. Working with so many talented writers locally is what sparked the idea for Deptford Literature Festival, which in turn prompted the Lewisham Borough of Literature campaign. And if the history of Spread the Word has taught us one thing, it's that a small idea for a project can snowball. So here's hoping for greater things across the next 30 years.

In the meantime however, we hope you enjoy reading these commissions and the 2025 Deptford Literature Festival, where you'll hear all of these pieces read and performed.

Ruth Harrison, Director
Spread the Word
March 2025

30th Anniversary Commissions

Emerging Writer Commissions

Theories of Change
Giselle Cory

There is no sense of a beginning or end. It moves like a river. I am nearly an hour late and have to walk against the crowd to find the group.

I squeeze past manicured older women who remind me of my mother, dogs wearing keffiyehs, and middle-aged men clustered behind a 'Scousers for Palestine' banner. Chants spring up and then fall away again, but I don't join in. I don't do anything. I've stopped walking, and am standing at the crowd's edge. Something is happening to me, but I can't name it yet. When I get home, I'll read that 300,000 of us came out, but for now, all I know is that there's an endless stream of people and many of them look like me.

I've settled on my identity but that wasn't always the case. The earlier iterations of me are still in there, with all their fear of being left out or worse. I am still the child who, upon realising I was different, fell into panic that others would find out too; who covered myself in sunscreen so I wouldn't *turn black* as my brother threatened I would; who picked up that *Palestinian* was a dirty word and didn't claim it in public. That child can hear people shouting *Free Free Palestine* at the top of their voices, in their thousands, and can see an endless patchwork of Palestinian flags and colours carried along by the crowd.

***

I scan for the group. I feel nervous to attach myself to strangers, but I didn't want to come alone. Dad had called as I was walking to the station.

'Hi. Listen. Are you meeting up with your friends there?' I knew where this was going.

'There's a group of us.' I don't tell him that we've never met. He'd find it odd that I sought out a group whose common thread is being in the minority. Of course, they look like the children of his friends, but he wouldn't claim that was by design. And he'd be surprised that he is my route in, that they would praise his otherness where he doesn't see any. Our parents unwittingly give us tickets to places, whether or not they want us to go there.

'Ok. Honey, I won't come today, if that's ok. It's… sometimes these things become antisemitic.' He says this last part quietly.

His hesitation doesn't surprise me. Growing up, I took pride in how little bitterness he carried with him. When he talked about the arrival of Zionist militias into his neighbourhood, I asked why the police did nothing. He paused before he replied, 'It was very difficult. They were having to put up with Arab *and* Zionist terrorism.' Recollections of the violence came with reminders that not everyone was in favour of it. When a family friend was shot coming out of his front door, Dad explained that a gang had taken over the house of the Jewish family next door, squatting at the windows with rifles and waiting for the man to leave for work. 'The family didn't ask the gang to come in. They didn't want any part of it. They just came, like in Northern Ireland.' But his benevolence has limits. 'A gang leader, a murderer, became Prime Minister of Israel,' he says with horror in his voice some 70 years later.

I thought him the wisest man alive and could only parrot his overtures. But today, his approach feels too small. And we can't both be right. If he's right, I'm naive or hateful. Striding towards the station, the years seem to be falling away like they were never attached at all, until I am a kid again, ashamed of falling short of the judgement of a parent.

'I obviously wouldn't be going if I thought that'd happen.' I hear how sharp I sound, and immediately regret it. 'But don't go if you're not comfortable.'

'If you can't find your friends, call me and I'll come and meet you.' I hear that he can protect me better than I can protect myself, and I flush with anger. It's only much later that I hear something else: a father wishing to protect their child, no matter her strength or his age. I tell him that I'll call him, but this is a lie.

***

From within the flow of the march, a woman shouts for my attention. I don't recognise her until she pulls down her N95 and waves me over.

The rest of the group and their pillar-box red placards resolve out of the crowd. The group is small and there's not much conversation. When it does come it's soon cut off by a megaphone. *Gaza Gaza don't you cry we will never let you die*. We are not here to chat, after all. I make a note to wear a beanie next time, hide an earbud underneath and listen to that podcast about real life hauntings.

The group all have keffiyehs or flags. I want to explain that Palestine isn't a brand for my family, that we don't collect insignia like it's a sports team. But in other ways I try to emulate them, desperate to fit in. I look the least other, and it makes me nervous. Unlike everyone else, I could pass as white – at least in London and if you didn't look too hard. In the noughties that felt like a gift.

I drop in that my father is Palestinian. It doesn't really help. They feel like pretenders next to me, and I feel like a fraud when someone says *I am so sorry*, like the war is hurting me more than it's hurting them, like I have any claim to pain or sympathy, like I know anything about what it feels like to be Palestinian.

***

The march slows as it navigates Hyde Park Corner. Someone climbs up a scaffolded building and raises a flag. Big cheers erupt. Up ahead, flares spew dirty smoke, short lines of green and red sitting in the damp air. I wish they wouldn't. It feels like opportunism, an excuse to be a bit naughty and get away with it. Protests are a spectacle. It's their purpose, but I bristle at the idea that we're all performing something together, every other weekend, almost like Church. But it's this or go to bed feeling like a spectator, as occupied territories are levelled. I find the spare placards stashed in the bottom of a buggy. I bounce one up and down in time with the chants, but say nothing. It feels too daring to say Palestine out loud, and bad manners to shout in public.

***

For an event Dad avoided for fear of violence, there are a lot of strollers. We come into step with a family as they crowd around one of their children. Someone hands the child a megaphone. After some direction from his father, he raises it to his mouth. His family erupt in celebration, and the boy gets louder and surer at each repetition.

I try to imagine my father passing on that life skill, but I can't. He's not the type to raise his voice. He taught me other things though. Growing up with images of the Second Intifada rolling on the little TV in the kitchen, of bloodied bodies, of grown men throwing rocks at tanks, I'd ask him for explanations. He would pause and explain some part of it, and we'd go on like this. We'd always get to a root 'why?' and he wouldn't have an answer. I appreciate this now, that he allowed for the perversity of the status quo and didn't try to rationalise the irrational just so he'd have all the answers, like some adults do.

He'd have made a good politician. He was a local councillor once, for the Tories. He still refers back to it now, 40 years later, because no experience since has felt more relevant or insightful. He saw how the sausages are made. A little while ago, I found an old Christmas gift tag at the back of a cupboard. A little square of paper with red and gold on one side and mum's spider crawl writing on the other. *To my little politician, love Wiffer.*

***

In 1948, the family lost their business, their homes, warehouses and offices, and their nation. Even their currency disappeared – the British Treasury withdrew the Palestinian pound as legal tender with a slender three months' notice. The business was mourned most of all, because it amounted to life: decades worth of days invested and lost.

My family intended to go to the US, but got as far as the UK. There they rebirthed the company in a three-storey store front in South London. It is still there, still trading under the family name though marriage means none of us go by that name anymore.

When Dad tells stories he says my brother's name when he means my great uncle, or replaces his mother's name with my mother's. He only does this when the people have done the same role – both risk-taking entrepreneurs leading the family, both administrators in the back office – as if those roles have been continuous over time, the individual people simply inhabiting them for a season.

I'm not in any of these roles. I do not exist across generations. My accolades sit like a jar of marbles. I was a CEO once, but it was in the charity sector. It doesn't count.

***

My father's father was able to remake his life by rebuilding his business. My father's mother had no such outlet. While he marked the passage of time through new contracts, new employees, new products, she stayed home. A stream of immigrants and exiles passed through the house, ever pulling her mind back to Haifa. She could not start again. She was lost to her loss, her bitterness covering her over like a crust. The day I learnt this about her, coaxed unwillingly from my father, I dreamt of a pipe, one end open to the air, the other stabbed into the earth. There is a body deep underneath it. I blow into it, trying to reinflate the buried woman back to life.

***

We turn onto Piccadilly. The Ritz, the Sheraton, the Wolseley. It's nearly Christmas and some of the hotels are sparkling inside, giving them a warm glow against the grey afternoon and the persistent, pathetic rain that slowly soaks through my coat. Staff stand in entrance ways, looking nervous, defiant or just annoyed. They watch us like we are a fanged snake that might turn and strike at any moment.

Bobbing my placard over the crowd gives me a little confidence, and soon enough I am shouting just like everyone else. I'm not sure where to look or who we are shouting at, but I feel awkward not joining in so I keep going, letting the sensation settle.

Among the chants of a *Free Free Palestine*, I feel false. I feel like I'm misleading someone. The solidarity is beautiful to witness. I'm glad to be here among this crowd and see such support for a place I was once scared to talk about outside the house. But permeating it all is a belief that resistance brings victory, despite so much history to the contrary. In his memoir *We Could Have Been friends, My Father and I*, Raja Shehadeh quotes Eliahu Sassoon, then a minister in the new Israeli government. 'Don't speak to me of justice, law, rights… these words have no place in our dictionary. It is power that determines the destiny of nations.' The history of Palestine since the British Mandate bears this out. And no matter our number today, we will not be heard by our Government. We have no power, save our embodied compassion. My fellow protestors seem to disregard history in favour of hope. My father is too much of a pragmatist to be here at all. I am caught between the two.

***

Sixty years on from the Nakba, we sought out the family's buildings in Haifa. We had trouble finding them. Towering billboards obscured the lot. They depicted a young woman with her finger to mouth, urging silence. I forget what she was selling. The buildings were still there, still empty, beautiful grey stone framing big windows covered with IDF-imprinted metal shutters. The door was ajar. We picked our way across a floor littered with needles, trying to breathe against the sour smell of human waste. The offices remained furnished as they had been, rotting papers on the tall bookshelves.

Even though the buildings remain, my father knows there is nothing to return to. Palestinian lawyer Muhammad Nimr Al-Hawari returned to his home as an Israeli Arab. 'It was as though I had come to a new country, not at all like the one I knew and had fought for.' Dad's country does not exist, anymore than his parents do. Ghosts, all.

***

At Piccadilly Circus, the usual backed-up traffic is gone, the whole square pedestrianised by the march. The fountain, normally a blackened bronze, is a pyramid of red and green, every climbable spot taken by boys holding flags. The passing protestors point and smile and take photos. I wordlessly disapprove. The statue at its centre is Eros, the god of passion who – writes its sculptor Alfred Gilbert – raises his bow 'sending forth indiscriminately, yet with purpose, his missile of kindness.' It's all we can do.

Rain trickles down my upheld arm and has soaked through my coat. My placard is rippled and flopping at the edges. The protest is so big that it moves slowly, in small shuffling steps and the lack of movement is leaving me shaking with cold. I wonder if it's acceptable to go home before we reach the end, but I decide against it. I'm caught between the grand arc of social justice and the small, immediate pulls of the body. I'd be too ashamed to let my discomfort win out.

Once we're at Trafalgar Square and the march is done, we huddle under the portico of the proud, old building that now houses Waterstones. Vendors tout watermelon badges, t-shirts, prayer beads. I am quick to say my goodbyes, but I don't go straight home. I want a buffer between this experience and home. I go to the Poetry Library on the Southbank and read Momtaza Mehri: *Diaspora is witnessing a murder without getting blood on your shirt.*

***

After dinner, Dad and I call up our cousin in Tel Aviv. She's old, unmarried and blunt. Where we expect sadness, we find inconvenience.

'I would like to go away at Christmas. To Egypt. I have a friend, we like to go away.' She relates some of the holidays they've been on together. 'With the war on, it might be difficult. But,' she says with a little smile audible down the phone, 'maybe I should be adventurous.'

One year later

We are taking our seats at the Royal Festival Hall. The room is warm and dimly lit as they introduce a series of speakers to reflect upon the life of Edward Said, a Palestinian-American academic and activist famous for throwing stones at Israeli tanks while holding a PhD from Harvard. He's long dead, but they say *A voice can be felt as much in its absence as in its presence* and immediately I feel his loss.

Dad settles in and I pass him his paper cup of black coffee. His eyes sweep the hall.

'All these people…' He looks around in awe, wide eyes giving him sudden youthfulness. He's not been on the streets, and activism gets little reported. How was he to know there had been a swell, that people were coming out for Palestine after so long?

We don't make friends, we don't smile and put our hands on each other's backs in welcome. This is central London. But we are here, we have come, we are reminded that there is a we.

***

They get our shame out early. A young, low-definition Edward Said comes on the screen: *…the humiliation of having to say We Do Exist.*

Said's life was shaped around questions of justice, but he also embraced exile. This is a knot: who gets to speak, how much distance makes you distant. He lived in New York City and said he wasn't sure he'd go back, even if Palestine was liberated. Exile had become life, so that he was no longer in exile. This was his success. His son is at the podium now, says he's not so sure his father would have stayed away, says it was an escape mechanism, that the father was protecting himself from heartbreak. Why are we, the children, so desperate for our parents to hold on?

It feels unfair to me that Dad and his parents got all the destruction and none of the credit for their own survival, and my generation, the second generation on, are handed microphones. We have not suffered, but are given all the nobility of oppression.

Perhaps this is because the second generation are the most familiar type of other. We belong, but we have good stories to tell, or perhaps re-tell. We carry our *home* culture but we fold it into British manners. We bring our difference as a gift, something offered, with none of the threat of our foreign-born parents. The second generation are ours but different.

***

Edward Said said *I came to the Palestinian cause not because I am Palestinian but because it is just.* My cheeks flush in the half-dark. I would not have come to this cause for justice's sake. Life is too heavy already. Had I been able to choose, I would not choose to hold this.

The rest is easier to agree with. A string of speakers tell us Palestine is the ground zero of liberal thought, that there is a battle for the Palestinian 'genre' to be categorised under righteous justice rather than terrorist, that history tells us partition – in any land, for any people – does not bring resolution. Dad falls asleep around speaker number three, his coat balled up on his lap.

Max Porter does a poetic monologue on his trip to the occupied territories. *What literary style beyond a scream can survive this moment?* Partway through, Dad's not-quite empty cup of coffee falls to the floor, jarring him back awake. When Porter is done, Dad leans over and says, a bit too loudly, 'I didn't think much of him at all.'

***

Towards the end, a Palestinian poet comes on, long curly hair coming down over his face. 'In resistance, you win if you do not disappear entirely,' he says. His voice is deep and seems to come from much further within than his mouth or throat. His big body is curved over the plinth. He lays out a chain of logic that ends 'And then they win!' for which there is loud applause. It wakes Dad, who joins in.

He leans over to me. 'Who wins?'

'The Palestinians.' I say this with too much disdain.

'I wasn't sure.' I am often angry with him these days, but it's not his fault.

The last speaker comes on, a slender woman who sounds a little embarrassed to be offering pragmatism after the roaring declarations of victory that came before her.

'The only recognisable feature of hope is action. Protest, boycott, write to your MP.' She lists successes – the BDS movement, arms protests including the Greek dock workers who blocked a shipment of arms to Israel – and applause erupts again. Dad doesn't join in this time.

***

The quote from Muhammad Nimr Al-Hawari is taken from We Could Have Been Friends, My Father and I *by Raja Shehadeh. Quotes from the 'Edward Said: The Question of Palestine' event at the Southbank Centre in November 2024: the poet is Tamim Al-Barghouti; the last speaker quoted is Ahdaf Soueif.*

Last Orders
Eliezer Gore

God's boredom has made him a comedian

The joke is me driving off a Scottish cliffside in a classic black and orange Benz. The trees caught me and threw me onto the H1. An angel pulls me over for driving while dead. I show him my mother's prayers that paid for this car. I speed past a lengthy pedestrian queue. Distracted by the sight of my grandma, I wave. She kisses her teeth or was it the skid of my tyres. My brakes aren't stopping. Actually there are no pedals. Dazzled by the light in my mirror. I am moved by the appearance of Jesus with my wheel in his hands.

A mother's short prayer

i
Almighty puzzle maker
God of storms and daughters

ii
Lord thy kingdom is full
with husband, son and prayer.
Am I poor enough?

iii
Is my heart too boastful in its weight
envy stirred from feathered lines on my skin.
I've learned to grow idle wings

The mourning after

                                                  No need to jump

Sorry mum

                    I opened the door

                                                        The knock was me

        Shook the graves in your skin

                            A slit of breeze

                                      I'm just beyond your window

      I'll pop back in

                Don't open the curtains

                                      Look, my ghost's on TV

I've finally learned transparency

Notes App

Mother's day gift
ticks to Zim?
zara black dress,
print pics of dad?

Movie idea #302
Rom com about a ghost and a mirror

6th form reunion guest list
T.j.
Honour
Renaya?

Plz buy
Silver tequila
Thank you cards

Dreams
sinking in sea of pebbles
margate ?
feet splash across water???
dads laugh as I'm buried in stones

If i ever get the money
Mermaids stole my uncle - THE MUSICAL

Send by Thursday (if you're bad)
I've left your keys by the green gnome.

Cheating the Sunday quiz

Hymn
is a religious song or poem of praise to God.

Mum says hands grow heavy from holding up whispers and the heart bursts through the throat.

Healing
is the process of making or becoming sound or healthy again.

I've seen it in practice: collapsing bodies scaffolded by hands.

Damned
are those condemned by God to suffer eternal punishment in hell.

Pastor doesn't believe in the word.

He told us not to wait for him as the world ends.

I'll be somewhere
hands muddy
chest hot
helping the damned up steps

Heaven is tired of hearing my father complain

I conduct a trial
in my therapist's office.
I steal my fathers voice.
It slips, landing where
my stomach retreats

I speak as my character witness
testify boys in hoods
watched me play dress up
and cheered me on

I brought my mother's pot
as evidence that sudza
is born from porridge

I conclude my father
would not approve
of me being here
when there are ears at home

Casting call

Unpaid supporting roles:

Spine: any age or race, this is the body's middle finger, stubborn, upright.

Mandem 1: black male 18-25, professional verbalist, rowdy pacifist.

Aunty Silvia: black female 40+, nurse who knows too much, sleeps on bus, must be bilingual.

▮▮▮▮: we are looking to see as many people as possible, we'll decide by process of elimination

God's boredom has made him a tough critic

[00:00:00]

Abi: Heaven what you saying, how we doing this eternity? South East of the kingdom, make some noise!

[00:00:13]

Abi: Ah, okay, maybe not everyone's risen yet. Whatever. Aight so hear this, Mum is at my grave, in the part of Zimbabwe the colonisers didn't find. I'm there, Dad next to me, we're laughing like the fish eagles circling Mum. What's funny is, Mum said we would run her into the grave first. But this aint that funny cause we won by losing the least.

[00:01:43]

Abi: Uh, so this other time, like wayback, like I'm 10 or 9, Mum is filming me and Dad, I'm wrapped in the blankets I wet two nights ago. I'm standing. Like I'm barely balanced, on one foot, with two candles in my hands. Uh, what's Dad doing again?

[00:03:19]

Dad is monologuing about discipline. I close my eyes and I remember my nightmares. Dad. Dad is reliving his dreams of being Denzel, my ears open and tears sneak up. They're marching down Dad's face and crawling out from under my eyes. Mum throws tissues, wah, wah, wah, like shooting stars escaping a war torn sky, she yells cut I think she got it.

[00:05:03]

Claps slow like newborn rainfall

[00:05:04]

Abi: Ugh, wait, please, um, Mum warned me if I stared at the screens too long I'd disappear into them. I open pages full of my face telling me millions of people have seen me a year ago, hundreds of comments asking if I'm still alive with no replies. so this joke starts with a blank screen. The page has been empty for months. This is not the day that changes.

To Ears and Tongues

Naomi Walsh

Sunlight warms my surface, leaves skimming across in quiet moments. The strangers beat me relentlessly. Shoes, cars, bikes. Bodies. Bare feet. I hold them up.

***

As Rach weaved amongst the traders and browsers, her heart maintained a fast flutter, settling high in her chest.

She reached the end of Deptford Market as her phone buzzed: *Should be there in 10.* She scrolled up to read the end of their last exchange at the top of the screen. *Have a nice life I guess.* Benji's assumption as 'the victim' in their breakup had led to explosive arguments since.

Sweat pricked under her arms as she strode under the railway bridge, the world darkening slightly. She hated being the one that had reached out, even if it was for the greater good. She was tired of always having to play nice. Fuck it, if she was honest she didn't want to do this.

Her vision went white. It was so blinding Rach instinctively closed her eyes, waiting for it to be over. Then she noticed the quiet. She slowly blinked her eyes open, pupils painfully contracting to adjust. Her eyes roamed left and right. There was nothing. Just white. Her breathing was the only sound.

'What the fuck?'

***

Loose change lends a metallic edge to the strangers' discarded chicken bones. Slicked with grease, little nibbles of crunch remain. Stale IPA trickles along my cracks.

***

The black cab beeped sharply at the hooded youth who had taken a wandering step off the pavement.

John tutted, the youth whipping his head to stare accusingly at John for daring to interrupt his screen time. It reminded John of who he was driving towards. Did he peer into black cabs and search for a familiar face? Or avoid looking into them, never hailing them, lumping all cabbies into a category of deadbeat: cannot be trusted.

The call had come in two weeks ago and John had been working more hours than usual to pass the time. Now it was here, and his head was spinning. Questions, theories, what ifs. He liked to live in the moment, but that felt hard when there was 20 years of history perching on his shoulder like a feral parrot, pricking his ear with doubts. If he'd had his way, he would have picked him up and taken him somewhere he needed to go that day. Preferably at least a 20 minute drive, which wouldn't be that hard to achieve in London traffic. Kills two birds with one stone, he appears helpful, and they could chat in the safety of the cab.

John made the turn onto Deptford High Street and slowed as he saw the barrier closing the road to the market. *Shit*, maybe this was a sign. He should rearrange. What's another week to get his head straight? Wrestling with the decision he passed under the railway bridge to turn around.

He slammed on the brakes as a white light blinded him.

***

I savour the summertime air. A gentle breeze wafts sweet jerk smoke along me. It tangles with burger onions, wrestles with fish guts.

***

This was a really weird dream, Rach thought. She focussed on that feeling. Always did when whatever was happening just couldn't be real. There was only one time that hadn't worked, and it was when a girl on the dancefloor had grabbed her face and kissed her and the whole world had stuttered on its course. This dream was the second.

Eyes snagging on something in the distance, she slowly walked towards it. The park bench was old but clean and looked so odd resting on the white floor without casting a shadow, as if she were in a photography studio.

The dedication plaque in the middle had faded with age. *To ears and tongues.*

Questions swirled around her head as she turned to inspect the bus stop pole next to it. Craning upwards, her stomach tightened as she read the stop name. *The Gap*. The 'towards' section below that was blank.

What now? Sit and wait for a fucking bus?

She froze at the distant sound of brakes squealing, then jumped back as a black cab wheeled into The Gap. The driver kept his hands on the wheel, eyes straight ahead. Rach strode over to knock on the window. The man turned his head to look at her before his hand slowly moved to press the window button.

'Greetin– hello. Are you here to… collect me?' The man just stared, his blank face unnerving her. 'I'd like to go to Deptford. Please.'

The man blinked. Swallowed, and finally seemed to focus on her. 'Where… the *fuck*, am I?'

Her budding hope crumpled like tissue paper, 'Fuuuuuck.'

The man got out of the cab and looked around, emotions flitting across his face. Confusion, fear, wonder. He finally turned back to her. She couldn't hide her disappointment as she explained, 'I thought you might have been part of it.'

'Part of what?'

'I don't know, whatever this is.'

The man frowned at her response. 'Could just be a glitch. Like in that space film.'

Rach opened her mouth to ask which film and then closed it. They were wasting time.

John appraised the girl in front of him as they swapped names. She was pretty. Not that he'd say that. He was about twenty years into the 'it's weird if you compliment younger women' territory. But her smooth, deep skin, long braids and even lips reminded him of someone else. 'What's with the bench?'

Rach sighed. 'I don't know, but it's real. Weird plaque too.' She studied him. Why would they both be brought here? They didn't seem alike. 'My phone can't make calls. I've wandered around but there's nothing else. The bus stop calls this place The Gap. That's all I know.'

'You sound like you're in detective mode.'

'Well, we want to get out, right? Maybe we triggered this, or we have something in common. If we figure it out, we might be able to leave. We can't be trapped here, we'll die.'

Her assumptions weren't quite as appealing as her appearance, John thought. 'Who knows what the laws of physics are here sweetheart, it's all a bit…' He waved his arms around to demonstrate. 'We might not need to eat or drink. We'll know soon enough because my stomach's like clockwork.' He patted his stomach, smiling, although he did feel a pang of fear. One of them had to keep it light, though.

She felt like screaming. 'Look, I've been here for a while and you're the first thing that's happened. We have to try something. Like, why us? So, where were you before this happened?'

He thought if she frowned any more her eyebrows might connect permanently. 'Alright, I hear you. Well, I was just driving through Deptford–'

'Under the bridge? Me too! What were you doing?' That made much more sense to her; geographical connection, not personal.

He rocked his feet from heel to toe, hands on his hips, avoiding eye contact. 'Just driving, nothing out of the ordinary.'

'Just… driving? Could you be more specific? Where were you driving to?'

'Hang on, how come it's all about me? What were *you* doing?'

Rach shrank back at the question. Then sighed in resignation, 'I was going to meet my ex.'

'Ah, matters of the heart. It doesn't get easier, I'll tell you that for free.' In his experience, it had only got more complex. More time for really inconvenient things to happen.

'Thanks, that's encouraging.' But she unfolded her arms.

Bingo, he thought. 'I hear a lot of stories from strangers, y'know, if you want any advice.' He'd always been partial to a bit of gossip.

'I doubt you'd have much to say about my story.'

'Try me! I've had the whole of London in my cab. Every type of break up. Fresh, old, bitter… scandalous.'

'What about women who realise they're into women and have to tell their boyfriend?'

'More common than you'd think, poppet.' That wasn't strictly true, but the art of cabbie conversation meant that you reaffirm what the punter is saying.

The reaction surprised her. She turned to flop on the bench. 'My ex, Benji, took it badly. Especially when he ran into me on a date in Peckham. And it's unfair for our friends to juggle us because we can't stand to be in the same room. So I messaged him to start the peace treaty.'

'It all sounds very complicated. Lots of rules and expectations.' He offered a grim smile. 'My view has always been that everyone should focus on their own life.'

'Well, we can't always focus on ourselves. If everyone did that it'd be a pretty sad society. You're a cabbie, you must help people every day?'

John didn't think she'd understand his bubble theory. In his cab, he controls a perfect bubble. Lights turn green. He drops off and is hailed down. He chats when needed, he doesn't when he's not. But when he steps out of the cab, John finds it difficult to negotiate the world. He can't connect with others, he doesn't know who he is. The proverbial bubble bursts.

'C'mon, John,' she pushed, 'there must be people you care about! Don't you have a family?' He hesitated. *Shit.* Maybe it was a touchy subject. She'd just shared though, and the silence turned intimate as she held his gaze.

***

A throng of busy strangers undulate around my market, flitting close without touching like birds in a flock. Kind ones stop to pet the cat. It remains a statue, keenly watching the pigeons peck my surface.

***

Stacey's mouth was so dry. She slipped into Sainsbury's for a five finger discount on a can of Coke. The security guard eyed her up, but she knew he wouldn't lift a finger. Why should he, on minimum wage? One nicked can wasn't going to bring down a supermarket.

The sugary bubbles surged down. She'd stay somewhere else tonight. Danny's shit D'n'B playlist was repetitive and he didn't have a scrap of food worth pilfering. She'd managed to swipe a baggie off the table when he wasn't looking, though.

She jolted as her leg started vibrating. She ignored it.

Her leg buzzed again. She couldn't have a moment of fucking peace these days.

'Mum, what now. It's not a good time.'

'It never is with you anymore. But I'm here, Stace. I still care. I'll make you a bacon butty all crispy like you like it.'

Her stomach grumbled. 'I don't have your money yet.'

'It's not for that! Can we not even *see* each other any more?'

She stalked back up the high street. 'I know what you're going to say and the answer is no. You don't have a spare room, and Darren fucking hates me.'

'Alright, alright. But please come over.'

She stopped and closed her eyes. 'Okay. I'll be half an hour.' She hung up as she reached the railway bridge, already regretting her decision.

A bright light burned her eyes. She screamed.

***

Fruit and veg deals are shouted. Followers of God proclaim His love. The new jazz night earns an 'oooh'. Butchers' knives thump out of sync. My complex symphony cannot find a tune.

***

'I don't… have a family. I almost did.' John chewed over the words, unfamiliar in his mouth. 'Shannice was gorgeous. Jumped in my cab and we chatted up a storm. Instant connection, so they say. I'd stop by hers when I clocked off. Then she started asking me why I'd never settled down. Perks of the job, I told her. I was too old for all that. One night I walked in and she was in bits, passed me a damp bit of paper. I saw those two lines and walked out without saying a word.'

'You were going to meet her?'

'No… him. My son found my number on his mum's phone. He's called Callum. He's 23.' He stared off into the liminal space around them, his fisted hands gently pulsed by his sides. It felt so strange to say the story aloud. The words forged a deep new bond in his flimsy life. *My son.*

Rach tried to muster the acceptance John had offered her. It wasn't right, though, for John to have walked away. *Selfish prick.* But hadn't Benji called her that?

They both peered skywards as a faint screaming sounded.

***

The strangers seem restless. They bump and scrape like boats hitting land. Night falls, and packs are formed to move along me. A lone wolf looks close to his last breath.

***

The burning light subsided and Stacey spun around to see two figures in front of her. The yuppie jumped back, eyes wide. The geezer reached forward to grab her arm, cutting off her scream.

'It's alright, we're not going to hurt you. You're safe. Well, relatively. We're a bit stuck.'

Stacey shrugged off the geezer's touch and rubbed her lank blonde hair out of her face. She took in the nothingness around them.

The yuppie stepped forward. 'We think we're here because we're connected somehow. What were you doing before you got here?'

'Who are you, the fucking police?' Stacey folded her arms.

'Look, I'm just trying to figure out how we get out of here. It's okay if it was something… bad.'

'What the fuck's that supposed to mean?' The yuppie took a step back again.

The geezer stepped in. 'She didn't mean it like that love, she's just a bit keen.'

After a beat, Stacey lowered her arms. They *did* seem harmless. They swapped names.

'Were you near Deptford railway bridge? Just before you came here?' said Rach.

Stacey met her eyes, then let out a breath. 'Yeah, I was on the phone. Then a bright light – that was it.' She drifted over to the bench, hand hesitating before resting on the wood.

'Were you… headed somewhere you wanted to go?'

Stacey's grip tightened on the bench. 'No, I wasn't.'

Taut silence settled around the three. Rach cleared her throat. 'I think I've got it. It happened when we were headed somewhere we didn't want to go, right? But now we're stuck here instead.' Rach looked upwards into the depthless white. 'I think it's to make us feel grateful for our lives.'

Nothing happened.

***

Some want to change me. Others cling to my history. They scoff at each other. I linger in the fissure between their desires.

***

Stacey cracked into laughter, which echoed as she doubled over the bench. 'Nice speech babe, what were you expecting, a round of applause?'

John spoke before Rach could answer. 'I don't think there's a big 'reason' – like a lot of things in life. This has just… happened.' His voice had a faraway character.

'No, that *can't* be right,' said Rach, her voice cracking. 'Everything has a reason. Otherwise what's the point in all this?'

Stacey straightened. 'I'm sure you're the type to have life wrapped in a bow, but I don't feel particularly grateful for my life. Maybe we're here as some kind of punishment.'

Rach felt something like shame prickle through her. 'I'm sorry about your life, I wish–'

'Save it. I don't need pity from people like you. Who say they care but never help.' Stacey spat back. The air hummed with tension.

'We've been sharing some pretty deep stuff in here.' John's voice was soft with invitation. 'Care to join us?'

Stacey picked at a tiny splinter on the bench. *To ears and tongues.* The silence became a soothing touch. 'I was talking to my mum. She wants to help, but I've let her down too many times.' Stacey's throat caught and squeezed. 'My flatmates kicked me out because I couldn't find another job. Too principled, they said. I went from helping the homeless to… well. I manage. But I've picked up some bad habits. And now I can't… stop.' Her gaze hardened and focussed on the mid distance. *Detach, don't think about it.* Her treacherous mouth opened again. 'I'm so… embarrassed. I don't know how to get back.'

A hand touched her shoulder. Stacey looked up to see John's silvered eyes. The empathy in his face lapped at her like a soft wave. It wasn't sharp, like pity. It felt warm, like a hug from her mum.

Rach considered them both. These two strangers' stories, so different from her own. Her precious answers floated into nothing.

She asked a question, instead. 'How do you think we get out?'

Silence settled again, for a while. Stacey considered. 'We're so different, there can't be a pattern. We must have passed each other a hundred times on that high street and never been more than strangers. If this hadn't happened, I wouldn't have spoken to either of you in my life. But I'm glad I did, for what it's worth.'

The three strangers looked at each other. Understanding passed like a torch to light their eyes. They slowly took steps to face one another. Rach's tears traced wet veins down her cheeks as she held out her hands. John gently took one as the lines of his face settled into calm acceptance. Stacey's eyes shone with hope as she connected the circle. A flash of light swept across their vision.

30th Anniversary Commissions

Deaf and Disabled Writer Commissions

Accepting Dirt as Tenderness: Love, Depression and My Community Garden (In Three Parts)

Oli Isaac

'Everything is gestation and then bringing forth. To let each impression and each germ of feeling come to completion wholly in itself, in the dark, in the inexpressible, the unconscious, beyond the reach of one's own intelligence, and await with deep humility and patience the birth-hour of a new clarity [...] There is no measuring with time, a year doesn't matter and ten years are nothing. Being an artist means, not reckoning and counting, but ripening like the tree which does not force its sap and stands confident in the storms of spring without fear that after them may come no summer.'

—Rainer Maria Rilke, *Letters to a Young Poet*

The thorn from the rosebush I cut back is lodged, tauntingly, under my skin. Every morning in the shower, it stings – a flash of pain in my thumb, then nothing. My girlfriend says it will work itself out eventually, but I wonder if it's stuck there for good. Like so much else in my life, it is neither healing nor breaking free, just existing – there – beneath the surface. I blame the cold.

1/ the soil under my fingernails [accepting dirt as tenderness]

My relationship with the garden begins, of course, with a romance.

It is January, 2023. Heidi, once a pen pal, then a lover, then a best friend, returns to my life after a six-year absence. By some strange fate, we are living on the same street – one of London's many thousands – and it feels inevitable when we immediately start dating. Evenings are devoted to long walks through Camberwell side streets and getting lost in darkening parks. We sketch the lives we lived without the other, holding hands that have long gone numb. Weekends are the gurgle of a coffee machine in the morning, the simmering of an evening shakshuka, my cat's wariness and curiosity. Then, one Sunday, Heidi invites me to a community garden.

She tells me she's been volunteering there for years. She says it'll make the South-East feel more knowable, offer a way to make it mine, six months after moving. But I make an excuse and decline the offer. I don't know anything about gardening, I tell her. I grew up in Dublin and Zagreb, playing on concrete; nature reduced to a grass football pitch. Every houseplant I own is either dead or barely hanging on. And besides, my vision of a community garden is bleak, a blur of passive-aggressive, elderly allotment politics and corporate team-building exercises. Spending a freezing afternoon there is not my idea of a date. But when she asks me for the third weekend in a row, I relent. Curious about her world, I now see the invite as a quiet gesture, welcoming me in. I show up near the end of a session, unsure of what I'm walking into.

On the way there, I cycle through Burgess Park, a patchwork of reimagined green space resting between Walworth, Camberwell, and Peckham. First proposed in 1943 in the wake of the Blitz, this 'green lung of South London' is a post-industrial anomaly – a rare instance of city sprawl in reverse. Rows of terraced houses, along with pubs, factories, and churches, were bought up and demolished, in a slow decades-long drip. By the 1990s, the radical and controversial plan had forcibly displaced around 30 streets, crafting 140 acres of shared public parkland in its place, piece by piece. Sitting on the edge of the park, Glengall Wharf Garden lives on the site of an old refuse depot. Here, London's rubbish was once loaded onto barges, which made their way down the Surrey Canal, a waterway long since drained and buried, and now transformed into a cycle path. At 14 years old, the community garden is well established – home to food-growing beds, hugel mounds, polytunnels, a forest garden, a chicken coop, and beehives. Its concrete foundations have been mulched and woodchipped into life. Like much of London, it is a place of dereliction and transformation, of things paved over, uprooted, and remade.

When I walk my bicycle through the gates for the first time, I don't know where to stand or how to belong. A couple of people hover over flower beds, offering brief smiles before their gazes return to the plants. Heidi runs over when she spots me across the garden. She laughs and mentions that the session is already ending for the afternoon. People are packing up the tools and collecting a harvest to take home – *'but thanks for coming.'* A volunteer named angel, also here for the first time, asks if we can help carry some wood back to theirs for shelves they are building. They offer in return a slice of freshly baked apple cake. It is the first of countless meals the three of us will share.

By the time spring arrives, I am committed. The garden is now a Sunday afternoon ritual, a quiet anchor in my week. When spring gives way to summer, the place hums with life, and the air is thick with warmth and movement. A rhythm takes hold, in sync with the season's abundance. I lock up my bike, make a round of hugs and hellos, then slip into the fold. I scoop frogs from the drying ponds, haul full watering cans across the beds, ferry the chickens from coop to pen. Faces take on names, names into stories – fragments of pasts, frustrations, small victories, and bad dates are scattered across our conversations. Sessions become a series of catchups over seed trays and beneath fruit trees, hands in the soil, roots entangling. The garden becomes a comfort, a community.

All of this unfolds without the exhaustion that comes with sustaining a modern cross-borough friendship: the strain of Google Calendar acrobatics, the quiet, nagging guilt of unread WhatsApp chats. Here, presence is fluid. People drift in and out – here one week, gone the next, but inevitably returning, if not for a Sunday session, then for fireside songs or spontaneous fundraisers. The casualness of garden camaraderie both belies and enables the strength of friendships and community that have become the bedrock of the garden experience. It is precisely this ease – this looseness – that allows something deeper to take root.

The garden, too, invites a different way of being and being with. Tasks are slow and repetitive. The compost bays always need turning and trugs of greens always need chopping. Again and again. For the uninitiated, boredom can creep in: the restless itch of being without distraction. But the garden asks us to attend: to the droop of a thirsty plant, or the suddenly-deepened purple of the artichoke flower. Given time, the mind softens. Boredom gives way to observation, then reflection, then something deeper still. The work becomes a meditation. Attention spills over into conversation – less transactional than outside the garden's boundaries, freer, lighter, gentler. The garden rekindles something rare – a space for connection that is effortless and unforced. It is a place where conversation can still arise unbidden, like green shoots after rain, or forgotten seeds in the wormery.

This self-organised, volunteer-led garden is a quiet defiance of the logic that understands land as commodity rather than commons. Here, the earth is not something to be owned or extracted from, but tended to – a living system to be nurtured. It is a gift of a place – radical in its generosity, political in its refusal to accept the given order of things. The world insists on its own inevitability: rents will rise, communities will be displaced, winters will be colder, protests will shrink. But the garden reminds me that nothing is fixed. The ground can be broken and remade; a place for redirecting rubbish can harbour foxes, mycelium, nasturtiums: uncountable stirrings of life. The seasons change, and what seems dead blooms again.

The garden thrives not by bending nature to its will, but by working with it in tandem. Beneath this lies the philosophy of permaculture, a way of tending to the land that can be traced back to Indigenous and traditional land practices. Permaculture gardens mirror the resilience and self-sufficiency of natural ecosystems, allowing nature's impulses to flourish. Nothing is wasted, and everything returns to the earth in time. It is making the most of what's already there.

The garden practises a *mantra* of minimal interference, refusing traditional horticulture's division of plants into 'good' and 'bad'. Most 'weeds' are left undisturbed, respected for the structural benefits they bring to the soil, and the way they provide groundcover and keep life circling. Uses are found for the few plants that are removed. Nettles are made into soup, borage is soaked and turned into a fertiliser, the bramble forms a thorny mulch under the crabapple tree.

The compost heap, a heaving pile of stems and scraps, holds the memory of past harvests and the promise of future ones. Rainwater is caught and saved before it slips into drains. We plant beans to fix nitrogen for the beds that will follow; in summer, they climb sweetcorn, and are nourished by a soil shaded by squash's broad leaves: the 'three sisters' growing in harmony. We mulch the soil to retain water and stop erosion, sow wildflowers to draw in pollinators, and when the growing cycle of each plant completes, save its seeds.

At the heart of permaculture are three ethics: care of the earth, care of people, and the sharing of surplus. In the garden, this means that everything is connected; that the whole is greater than the sum of its parts; that every action is deliberate. Decay is not an end but a beginning, the waste of one system can be the nourishment of another. Permaculture is not just a method but a message: renewal is always possible. In a city where green space is constantly threatened by developers, the garden insists on this – not as nostalgia, but as adaptation.

My gardening know-how remains stubbornly lacking, but my world has widened. My way of being has burst open. Outside the garden, the logic of my life is governed by a relentless need for achievement as a measure of self-worth, and the concomitant pressure to constantly be moving forward, where time is measured in deadlines, where my day is a desperate scramble of to-do lists and a punishing hour-by-hour daily plan. Productivity smothers a depression that threatens to erupt if I dwell too long inside my own mind. It keeps the engine of my body and brain running until it exhausts itself.

But garden teaches me another way. Things get done but they are *not* hurried. There is time to linger. And in that lingering, I notice what I might otherwise overlook: steam rising from the compost heap on cold mornings, an iridescent rose chafer navigating the ridges of my palm, the soft give of woodchip underfoot after rain, the ethereal sway of a calendula in a breeze, its golden head tilting toward the sun. My gaze settles on small, shifting details and the world slows. Time stretches and loosens its grip, and drifts out of view.

'Perhaps our most serious cultural loss in recent centuries is the knowledge that some things, though limited, are inexhaustible,' writes Wendell Berry. 'A small place … can provide opportunities of work and learning, and a fund of beauty, solace, and pleasure – in addition to its difficulties – that cannot be exhausted in a lifetime or in generations.' The garden embodies this. It does not demand attention the way the world outside does – through notifications, alerts, obligations. It draws attention through presence, through patience.

Gradually, I begin to understand that stopping to name a plant is its own quiet kind of rebellion, some small but potent refusal of the attention economy. The American poet Mary Oliver once wrote, 'Attention is the beginning of devotion'. But, in a world where our time and attention have become resources to be mined and monetised, what are we devoted to?

Writer Michael Sacasas, on his Substack *The Convivial Society*, describes the modern digital-led culture as 'a great engine of desire, training us to want what it offers and encouraging us to forget our deep desire for that which cannot be bought.' He calls ours an era of depletion, where life's boundaries have thinned, where 'we are always on and always available,' where human and non-human alike are treated as raw materials, as sites of extraction. The result?

> *The arc of digital culture bends toward exhaustion. When we think of the way our days are structured, the kinds of activities most readily on offer, the mode of relating to the world we are encouraged to adopt, etc. – in each case we are more likely to find ourselves spent rather than sustained. The default set of experiences on offer to us are more likely to leave us feeling drained and depleted rather than satisfied and renewed. In our consumption, we are consumed.*

The garden, by contrast, is a space of renewal. A place where time is not hoarded or spent but lived. Where progress is not linear, but cyclical, untidy, slow. It is no coincidence that Bill Mollison, one of permaculture's founders, framed it as a philosophy of resistance against capitalism and industry, a reimagining of how we live and relate to the world. Novelist and philosopher Iris Murdoch writes, 'Reality is that which is revealed to the patient eye of love.' To stop and notice – to truly notice – is to resist. It is to reclaim a piece of ourselves from the relentless demands of productivity and consumption. You cannot rush seedlings into bloom or will the rain to fall. You simply have to tend to what is there and trust in time.

In her book *How to Do Nothing: Resisting the Attention Economy*, the American multidisciplinary artist, Jenny Odell, describes time as 'an economic resource that we can no longer justify spending on nothing'. In a world engineered towards constant productivity, that demands an endless growth, 'doing nothing' – like spending an afternoon among people and plants – can be radical, and subversive against an encroaching neoliberal consensus that insists all time must be productive. Odell contrasts horizontal time – the linear, forward-driven time of work and progress – with vertical time, the kind that stretches time into something more. A minute spent immersed in a book or watching a tree sway is different to a minute spent on a screen. The garden is a gift of time returned to itself, one that replenishes rather than depletes, nurtures rather than extracts.

We sit over communal lunch, cooked by volunteers, with soil-smudged hands and sweaty shirts, catching up and being there, fully. These small acts of community ripple out. In the promise of permaculture, the garden isn't a place where growth happens in isolation; instead, it develops into a place where relationships flourish: between species, between people, and between the land and its cadences. Bonfires are lit, solstices and equinoxes celebrated. Folk nights are held, a sauna moves in, yet another volunteer quits their job to become a gardener, we host fundraisers for Lebanon, for Gaza. Friendships spill beyond the gates, reshaping the city itself. Sacasas writes, 'By our attention we gain the world and the world becomes a home.' This is precisely the gift that Glengall offers.

***

2 / the sun sets before 4pm and ice lines the gutters [fallow & forgotten]

It is my second winter at the garden. Where once forty volunteers gathered in summer, now only five or six remain by mid-December. Bitter winds sweep through the beds, through coats, through bone. Sunlight, when it comes, feels all the more precious; a fleeting kind of gold. The vibrant noise of the summer has drained away, leaving only the caw of a crow, the routine rustle of bare branches. Like clockwork, sparrows flit tirelessly back-and-forth between two now-naked trees, indifferent to the humans below. The smell of wet soil after another bout of rain. The sharp crunch of untouched frost underfoot, revealing traces of fox tracks in the morning. Even the chickens are quieter, their feathers fluffed against the cold. The work, too, changes – paring back to the essentials. It is layering mulch, saving seeds, pruning branches. All this is groundwork – the reward only visible months, even years, down the line. And at times, it's hard to see the point. It becomes harder to show up. As the temperature falls, people drop away, retreating into their homes. The ebb of collective energy. The fatigue of the last weeks of work before another year folds in on itself. Winter has a way of driving everything inward.

One December afternoon, I stand in the garden, oblivious to news reports of a named storm on its way, and I find myself, for the first time, miserable here. The life I face outside of the garden gates is barrelling in. And the feeling terrifies me.

I had hoped this winter would be a threshold – a space to step into something new. To dive into writing, to finally move towards long-postponed, long-neglected desires and calcified dreams. I had romanticised the season. Its restraint, its clarity. No riot of green, no sprawling vines. Just the bare bones of things. I thought it might be the season that saved me.

Instead, I am consumed by a relationship fraying at its edges, a pile-up of unexpected deadlines, a descent into depression. And it feels relentless. A line from my favourite Frank O'Hara poem comes to mind; I move through the world 'with the metallic coils of the tide around my fathomless arms'.

I look up and think: winter should be one of two things – crisp, frosty blue mornings, or days blanketed with snow. But not this monochrome sky. This unyielding greyness. Not the sun immured behind clouds. Not the freezing gusts, the second of snow immediately turning to sludge. December blurs. The days at the garden smudged together like the weather itself.

I think back to the start of November. A 'not guilty' verdict that had brought no catharsis. A resignation letter sent in the sterile quiet of my flat. A relationship beginning to falter under its own weight. The job was supposed to end, but the relationship was supposed to remain.

I had stood outside Stratford Magistrates Court, tasting anti-climactic relief alongside four co-defendants six months after we were arrested for stopping an immigration raid on a hotel in Peckham. The trial was meant to last two days, but when the day arrived, it was over within a couple hours: a farcically quick 'not guilty' verdict. The stress had been in the lead-up: navigating legal aid and endless phone calls with solicitors, the unknown-ness of the day itself pressing at the back of my skull for months. And yet, when it was done, there was no elation, just an absence where the worry had been. That same week, I quietly quit my job. It was a decision I had retreated from making for months. Days spent without leaving the flat had worn me thin. I had lived a decade of fixed hours and wages, but the safety of it, and the comfort of routine, had long turned stagnant: a wound I had let fester.

November got underway, and despite the lack of catharsis, I felt something close to hope. I held onto it as a starting gun – a moment to shed the millstones of stress that had hung around my neck for months. I would embrace unemployment as an opportunity to write. I had commissions lined up and I wanted to see if these could hold me afloat on the waves. I had a plan. I had also told myself that when I quit my job, I would finally take my gender transition seriously, after years of hesitation. That I would become a person I was proud to be – and comfortable being. For two years, I had been micro-dosing hormones – tiny cut-up pills swallowed every morning at placebo-level doses. It was the act of taking them that mattered more than anything. But then, in October, I attended a support meeting for those looking into DIY hormone replacement therapy and prepared to finally reach for something more.

I wanted to earnestly mirror the season: to strip things back, to lay the foundations of a new life in time for spring. And when those seedlings finally broke through the soil, I thought, the sun would feel so pure and kind.

But instead, a rupture. And then, an unravelling.

In the second week of November, Heidi returns from a trip. A comment is made, careless or deliberate, it doesn't matter. It is a moment where something is revealed, and once seen, cannot be unseen. A line crossed, a trust broken. A sudden lurch in my stomach, the quiet but certain knowledge that things will not be the same. The distance spreads – slowly at first, and then impossible to ignore. It lets in a flood of insecurities. Conversations turn brittle, apologies don't land. Arguments, circular and exhausting. I try to explain my hurt, but she meets me with something unreachable. The more I try to grasp for certainty, the more slippery everything becomes. We start couples therapy, as if it might help name what is breaking. My flat no longer feels like home, nor like it holds a future It feels like a space we are waiting each other out, but from the farthest edges of the room. Still, I keep going to the garden.

I begin writing late into the night, pouring myself into pieces of work that I refuse to finish. The exhaustion takes its toll. I tumble deeper and deeper into a darkness until I'm in freefall. After a decade on anti-depressants, I had stopped taking them earlier this year, convinced I was steady enough without them. But this old illness, lurking at the back of my head for half of my life, contaminates my thoughts like groundwater. Some days, I feel it before I wake – before the morning even arrives. The weight pressing at the edges of my consciousness. Soon, the promise of unemployment curdles into panic.

I tell myself I am too busy to see friends, when the truth is that I no longer know how to be with them. Still, I keep going to the garden.

The person I had envisioned is slipping away from me. Tomorrow becomes next week, becomes next month. The slipping feels permanent. A new life postponed and postponed until the gap between myself and the hope I clung to grows too great and shatters. I am untethered, unmoored and too tired to start again. What was meant to be a season of recovery became a struggle to stay afloat.

Despite it all, I keep showing up at the garden. Not because I want to, but because it is something to hold onto, though I don't know if this means discipline or just a failure of imagination. Showing up is what everyone tells me to do, day in, day out. TV shows. Therapists. An instructor on a breathwork course I abandoned after one session. Investment gurus on unskippable YouTube ads. I am reminded of something Susan Sontag once wrote – that we value suffering only when it is transformed into something else. Into art, or wisdom, or even just a story with a beginning, middle, and end. But what if suffering remains formless? What is the difference between endurance and being stuck? Between commitment and inertia? Between resilience and resignation? What if the showing up is just showing up? No redemption, no transformation.

As the storm approaches and becomes a real thing in the sky above me, this space of patience and tenderness begins to warp. Its borders crumble. The weight of my outside world seeps in. An unease bubbles up. I feel *in* my body in the worst possible way. The cold bites at my fingers until they feel like something separate from me, and the idling small talk over secateurs, once a gift, becomes intolerable. I want to be anywhere but here.

I sort seeds from the dried mallow for the next year. Gather up rose hips. Pour a hot mint tea. Welcome newcomers. I try to ground myself. And it feels unbearable. My mind is elsewhere, circling the life disintegrating outside this garden. I leave early. Walk past the rows of dormant cherry trees, past the shouts from the football fields. I sit by the man-made lake, drop my head into my hands and cry. Ducks and swans waddle past. Two men carry fishing poles. I wanted to be outside, to sit in these feelings, to let them wash over me in the fresh, open air – but I couldn't. Winter wouldn't let me. The freezing wind presses against my face. Relentlessly so. It did not mould itself for me.

And suddenly, I am afraid. Afraid that this space, this last refuge, had been infected with the same sameness that I felt everywhere else.

On the last Sunday before Christmas, I am told to saw thick branches of a beautiful rose bush – something only done every few years. My body uneasy and restless. I hold the old branches, pale and grey compared to the green of new growth, and hesitate. I know this act of bluntness will sustain it in the long run. But it *feels* wrong, severing something that has survived this long. I spot a winter raspberry among the debris, perfectly ripe, and slip it into my pocket. I leave with a rose thorn lodged in my thumb.

Within days, it is a faint red scab, a reminder with feeling. Heidi tells me it will work its way out on its own. Not to force it. But it stays in. The cold holds back the blood from my hands and slows down the healing.

And then, one day, just after the start of the new year, it vanishes from view and becomes part of me.

***

3 / a pale sun, a blue sky, and breath visible for a moment

It is February, 2025. Someone I follow on Instagram shares a passage from an obscure book they are reading, the *University of Spiritualism* by Harry Boddington (published by the aptly named Psychic Book Club in 1946).

> *Man is both an actor and a circumstance – a cause and an effect. He should be treated not as having will and power to do that which he desires when and where he pleases but he should be born, educated, situated, rewarded, punished as a tree – capable of yielding good fruit only when it is properly organised and conditioned in good soil.*

The person adds their own caption: *A sickly tree can't be punished into growth.*

At the garden, the numbers blossom from twenty, to thirty, to forty people, drawn in by the vague pull of self-improvement. Something in the air of resolutions, a collective need to start fresh by giving oneself over to community and earth. It reminds me of Judith Butler's idea of identity as something we perform through repetition, a series of small, deliberate acts that eventually become who we are. Maybe that's why I keep coming to the garden, even on the days I don't want to. Even when it feels pointless. Even when I'd rather stay in bed. I know it's in the repetition that a self roots – a sense of identity that doesn't slip through my fingers, built through muscle memory, a becoming in the midst of others. Each time I show up, I choose to believe in something: growth, connection, the possibility of change. Even in winter. My hands ache from the cold, but that ache pulls me out of my head. It reminds me I'm still here.

And so, I try again – to reach out to the life I long for, to the identity, the body, the work, loved and beloved. I step toward a newness, albeit more bruised and burnt from the remaining embers of the old year. I begin to write again, to imagine beyond the next day or two, to move through the world holding out my restless heart.

The garden spills over onto the page. These words I write and the seedlings that I watch grow both require the same quiet, steady practice of looking, tending, and waiting. In the garden, I attune myself to the subtle changes in the soil, the slow unfurling of leaves, the quiet warnings of decay. Whilst I write, I pay attention to the weight of a remembered silence, the way light falls in a familiar room, a shift in a voice that gives something away. It is in these moments that meaning emerges. Here, at my laptop, in the garden, I resist the urge to glance and move on. Instead, I hold a thing in my mind and turn it over until it yields something new, or reveals something deeper beneath its surface. There is the same deep attention, a willingness to sit with the world as it is, to listen, to absorb, to make connections. Without it, language becomes hollow.

Nothing flourishes without care.

I run my finger over the spot on my thumb where the thorn was, half-expecting to feel it again. Healing is like that, I think – quiet, unnoticed, never quite complete. A scab, after all, is not static; it works unseen, beneath the surface. With freezing hands, I am nurturing what cannot yet be pictured.

The branches I sawed down last month lie where I left them, their rough elastic fibres splitting apart, the debris of what once thrived scattered across the beds – an interruption in the slow, patient growth of the trees. A reminder that even the most resilient things must sometimes be cut back before growth can begin again.

I think back to when the garden could not hold me. Its usual embrace was distant, and its rhythms were out of sync with what I needed. Its silence, once grounding, felt stark. The work, once meditative, became mechanical. I had turned to it as a counterpoint to whatever was unravelling beyond its gates. But maybe I was asking too much of it, mistaking its steady cycles for promises.

When I first came to Glengall Wharf, I saw it as a sanctuary, a place where I could seal off the noise in my life. But now I wonder if that's the wrong way to think about it.

It doesn't offer escape.

It offers work. Sometimes hard, boring, thankless work, the kind that makes your hands ache and leaves thorns in your skin. The kind that feels pointless in the moment but means everything in the long run. An uneven flow of resistance and surrender.

Maybe that's what I need right now. Something to push against.

In the absence of light, I'm learning to strive for the small, deliberate acts of care that keep life going. Even in winter.

To my Great Aunty Beryl who didn't speak at first
Ellie Spirrett

Beryl, did you know what would happen
to your name when you died? I am still hanging
halfway out of my school uniform when mum
drops it into her cereal bowl.

*You know my Aunty Beryl, the one
who moved to Australia, she's
dead.* Then she pins the morning
down into her hair and lets the day
carry on like a shopping trolley
down a hill.

When I'm just outside the corner of her eye
I see the text from her sister. It bears your name
like skin after a ripped-off plaster
and pads it with cotton. *How's it going
busy over here, don't know if you've heard.*

Grandma buries you in her loft on the other side
of the world from your body, Beryl. Sometimes
on gin-soaked afternoons she rolls your name
across her mouth like a cough sweet
she wasn't supposed to eat.

I paste myself like wallpaper around the living room
with my sister, making space for the silence that chokes
the air. When everyone is asleep, we try
to paint it into a picture of the lady
we never met that sits on everybody's chest.
No one can afford the plane ticket to your funeral.

I learn of the men who gathered around your body
like mice in the bin, and toasted to you for keeping
their shoes tied and their beards full of mash
and gravy. Then they dragged their tails to the pub
and left your name in the tip jar for the staff to split
between them.

Nobody tells me your favourite colour,
or how hot you liked your semolina.

I know you through questions
that I've collected over the years like the old dolls
in the shed. Grandma says the two of you would lie,
ankles forming speech marks around each other's heads.
letting the night gather in the gaps between you.

She'd say, *Beryl, why don't you talk?*
and you'd answer by rolling your chin against the ball
of her heel. She kept her palms clean for you to touch.
She warned you about boys who pull hair in school.
She told you not to scream.

Grandma used to say I remind her of you, the way
my arms shake like the colours of a firework
and how my eyes never meet hers.

I remember how it feels to exist like that before
you are pulled down from the sky
by people who want you to be still.

So, I chuck out the image of your lonely funeral
and I make some space to build you a world
big enough to hold every explosion
that your body can think to form.

I give you a dinner table that doesn't snap
you up when you say the wrong thing.
In school, the kids never cut names
out of their workbooks
and tuck them into your joints.

Beryl, could anyone hear the pain in your walk
from those rules that sat in the ground
and detonated when you stepped too close?
Did anyone see where the shrapnel settled
in your ribs and sprouted into your bones?

I know that a body like this is easy to give away.
that muscles who are too busy trying to crawl
out of your arms don't usually fight back.

Grandma asks why you climbed onto a plane
with a man that ripped you out of your family
and stuffed you in his pocket.
She spits his name out like she's just managed
to dislodge it from her throat.

She says he knew how to make a bin liner of your voice
and fill it with his own. He knew how to overcook it
with just enough *loves* and *darlings*
that you would not stop eating it.
It would form a skin on your tongue
and clump in the back of your mouth like a fist.

She never asked you
if you had worked out which door
in your house would close the quietest.
Which neighbour would be most likely

to let you in, and not hand you back to him
like borrowed sugar.

I think of the photos bloating
inside envelopes in Grandma's loft
of your lips pinched into frowns.
You, embedding into your house
like a stomach ache.

No one asking about your favourite colour,
or how hot you like your semolina,
and I wonder at what point you forgot.

I try to clear more space, enough space
to give you another side of the world
with no men with pockets,
or recipes. But I still don't believe
in that side of the world.

So instead, I give you one room
where you can find yourself again.
You rip open the night with your arms
like you used to in your childhood bed
and the walls keep your secrets.

You pull out all of the dirt in your joints
like hair from a shower drain, taking
his voice with it until you only have your own.
In this room, you never die. Or when you do
it is loud and sharp and huge.

The last thing I have to give you is a new funeral.
My head becomes a church, dripping
in stained glass windows that stream sunbeams

across the hemispheres. The pews are stuffed
like meat into sausages with women who love you.

Their stories pile on your coffin
until we can't see it anymore. Everyone
holds a photo of you on their laps,
and your smile pierces their guts.
We spray each other with your perfume
until our wrists are full.

And afterwards we spill onto
the street like thick semolina,
smearing your name on every road sign.

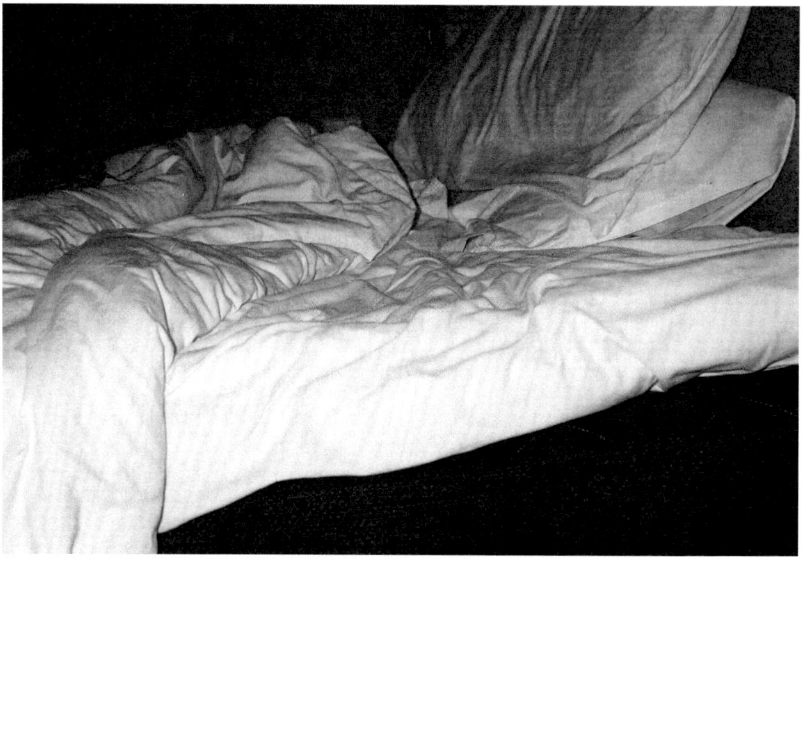

Flare: the muted outline of a body in bed as a camera flash overtakes the scene

Jamila Prowse

1. *Bed, the dominating character of this series, fills the majority of the analogue photograph. White, generic sheets are those of a hotel room. The bedding is indented with lines, the duvet pulled back in disarray and the pillows are squashed. No body is present, but there is a ghostly allusion to the weight of a human form. Adding to the haunting effect, the light pools against the auburn wall, producing a slight halo above the bed. The misaligned mattress, with its visible seams, regrounds us in reality.*

No one knows me better than my bed. Days, weeks, months and years, blur in the undefined passage of sick time. My imprint carved permanently into its contours. Sheets and pillows that understand me intimately. Bed: my constant companion. My closest confidante. To be sick is to succumb to it completely. The imminence of a crash forever looms on the periphery, threatening to overtake. My bed was an extension of my body – an extra limb – long before I spent a year fused to its surface. I never expected to become more disabled than I already was. For new barriers to sprout from the untended earth; unfamiliar, uninvited, unwelcome and yet here regardless. Insisting upon themselves.

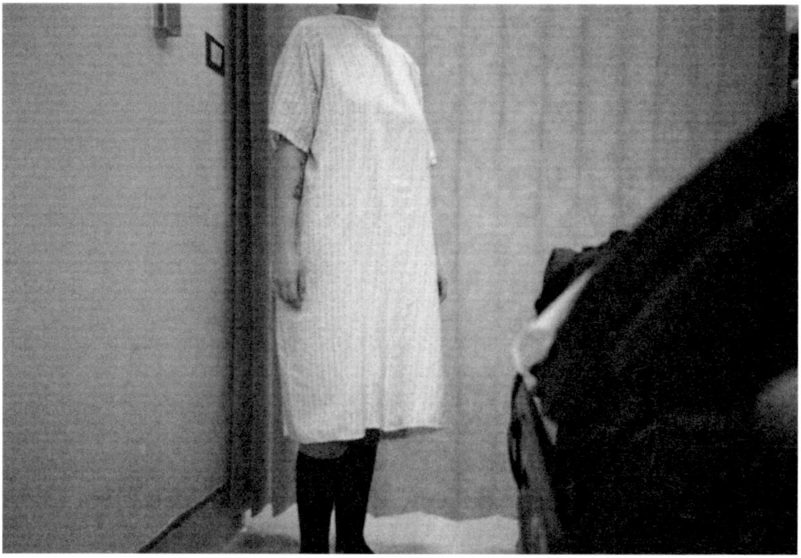

2. *A body, beheaded by the camera, stands in a small, partitioned cubicle. All identifying characteristics have been scrubbed by the medical attire of a shapeless gown and knee-high compression socks. Two uncovered arms hang limply from the billowing material. The wall on the left is bare, aside from a basic light switch, and the edge of an unidentified box. An out of focus mechanical bed protrudes from the right. A backdrop is provided by the luminescent green of a hospital curtain; the only vibrant colour.*

New symptoms appear, seemingly from nowhere. Each one is a domino falling into the next. Living in bed causes chronic back pain. I take high dose painkillers and develop digestive issues. When I wean myself off the medication for my unruly mind, I hallucinate the sound of knocking. I wake fitfully throughout the night, convinced someone is on the other side of the door. I peer through the peephole in anticipation of a visitor. The empty hallway stares me down, predictable as ever. Pain is a dulled heart monitor, thrumming. Muscles I didn't know could speak, fight to be heard above the constellation of complaining parts. My body doesn't belong to me. Did it ever?

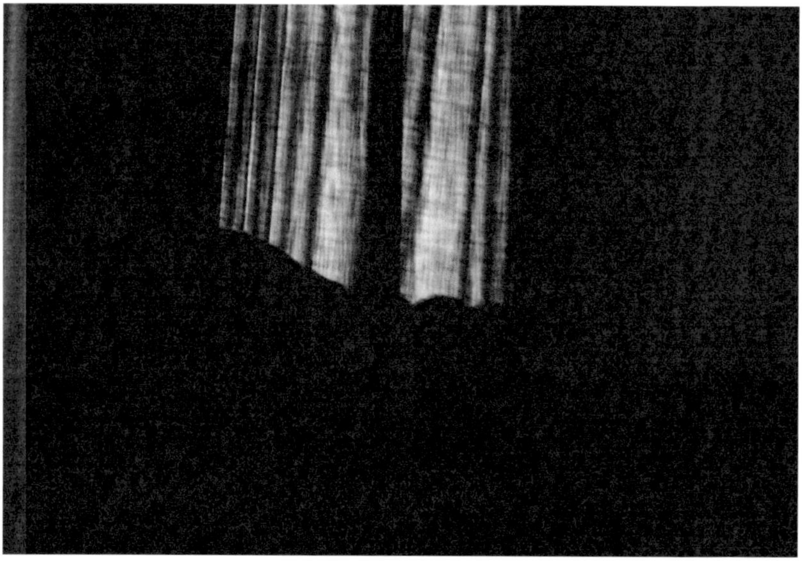

3. *Darkness descends, confronting us with an assortment of indiscernible shapes. The closed curtains shut out the only source of light, dappling a lined motif across the fibres of the material. Just beneath the veiled window is a curving, bumpy outline. Peaks and troughs could communicate the uneven terrain of a hilly landscape, but here, they are the intimation of a dormant body. Imperfections of dust speckle the image. A light distortion leaks vertically across the left-hand edge. The precariousness of film photography is akin to disability.*

A whole summer of bed. Never feeling the sun on my face, holding me with its gentle fingertips. I pull my curtains tight against the world. My own quiet protest. A refusal to let the outside infiltrate. It feels like mocking, the insistence to continue on without me. The sole marker of my formless days is the clockwork, ritualistic arrival of the ice cream van in the street outside. Seasonal sounds of freedom and play, drift in on the warm breeze.

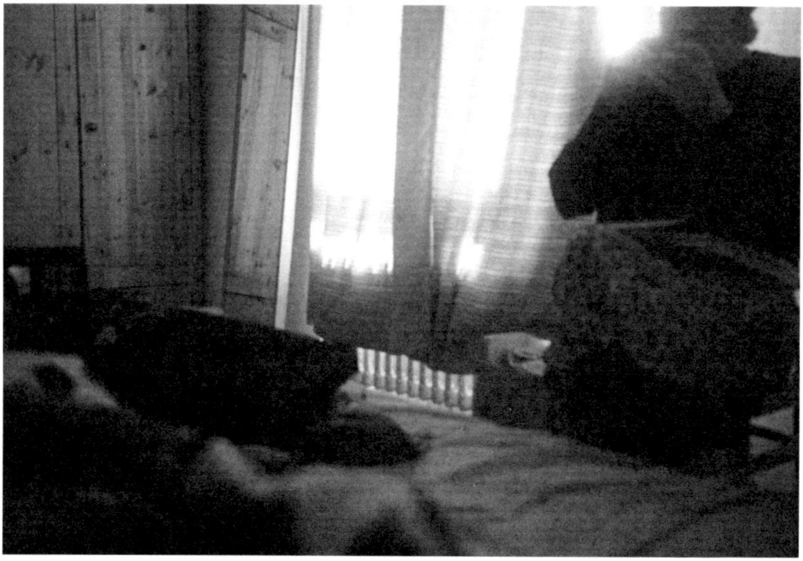

4. *We find ourselves in another room. Or is it the same one? Hard to tell. The curtains remain purposefully sealed. Whereas before, the light couldn't contend with the overwhelming darkness, here the sun is fierce, fighting through to illuminate the whole interior. Taken from bed, the edge of a mattress is busy with blankets and objects. A laptop screen is playing a film or TV series, though it's unclear what. Reflected in a vertical mirror is a wooden wardrobe. A bleary bedside figure sits in a chair next to the bed, wearing a bold, floral skirt and black jumper. Held in both hands, they place a sandwich into their waiting mouth, and in the process hide their face.*

To be cared for is to be witnessed in my most exposing, private moments. I dress in a uniform of the bedridden: old t-shirts worn with holes, pyjama trousers faded with overuse. My wardrobe is untouched. Moths feast in the crevices of stale fabrics. My mum didn't anticipate the ways sickness would reshape our lives, colouring it in an unforgiving greyscale of repetition. Her adult daughter, thirty years old, reverted back to the helplessness of birth. We crowd each other. We breathe the same air until the room is tight and gasping for relief. Once connected to the mainland, our part of the world gradually breaks off until we are an island adrift, suddenly too far for anyone to brave the voyage and meet us where we're at.

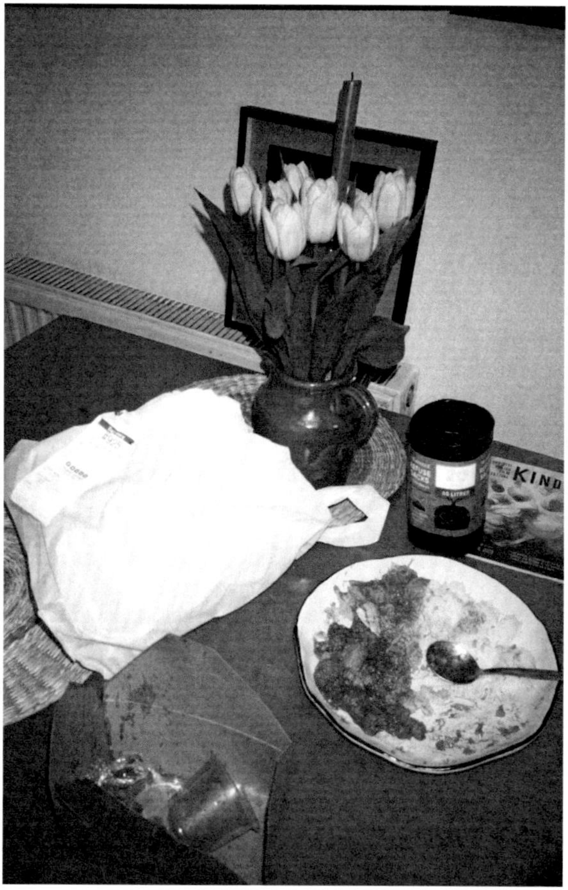
KIND

5. *During school days, teachers would pose uninspiring fruit in ceramic bowls to paint from. If the arrangement on the screen is comparable, it is by accident. Rather, objects have been abandoned at random, as they often are in a preoccupied household. Atop a midcentury dining table is a muddle of kitchen paraphernalia. Some decorative: woven, circular mats, a ceramic jug filled with fresh pink tulips which obscures an artwork. A candlestick emerges from the flowers, part of the bouquet. Ruining the impression of order are objects of mess. A roll of bin bags. Old, half eaten food on plates and in boxes. A plastic bag with a receipt stapled to it. Viewing only a corner of the room, the clutter appears manageable. Easy to clean up. Who knows what level of disorder lurks beyond the frame.*

A still life. Stilled life. The accumulated debris of a life unmanaged. Hinting at a wider scene. I exist, suspended, outside the realms of social acceptability. The washing-up piles high. Discarded food rots. Takeaway cartons stack haphazardly, a game of jenga. I await mum's next day off work, to restore order to the chaos.

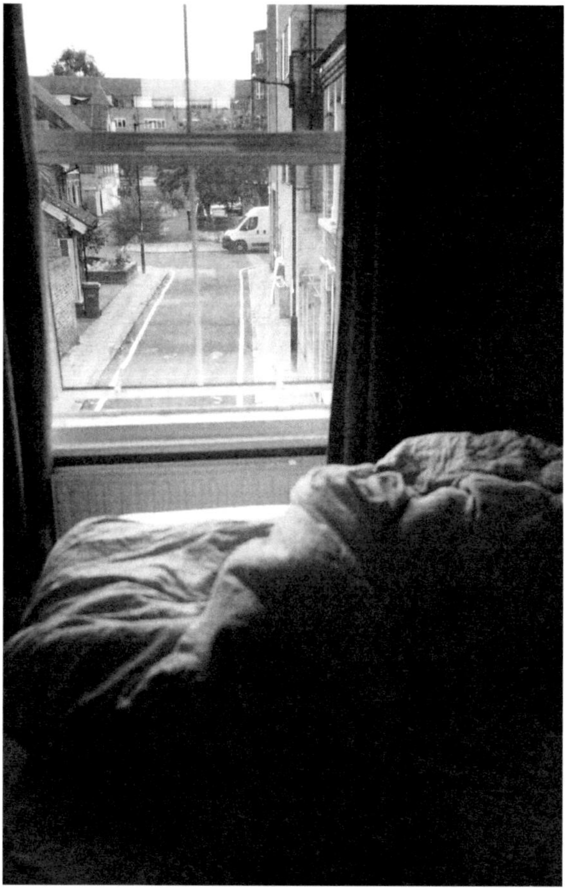

6. *Jumble of sheets, we've come to know you well. This time, in a pleasing, ochre linen. No space next to the bed for a chair; this is not the same room from earlier. Unlike before, the curtains are open to an empty street; typically residential with houses, a green wheelie bin, and a parked van. Single yellow lines demarcate the road. The photograph looks out while separated from the external world.*

A summer spent ferrying my ailing body between different beds, seeking refuge. Our little flat, gifted to us thirty years ago, when social housing still hung a safety net to catch our fall. It became inaccessible overnight. Planes trace chemtrails directly above, so when I stand up straight the crown of my head disturbs their foamy paths. Trains rattle our foundations. And all at once I cannot cope. I stop sleeping. I scream against the noise, adding to the atmosphere of unrest. A friend offers her home as sanctuary. I find somewhere else to lay my head, exchanging the steady caress of one mattress for another. If I listen closely enough, I can hear the reassuring pulse of a kindred crip body, beating softly through the wall.

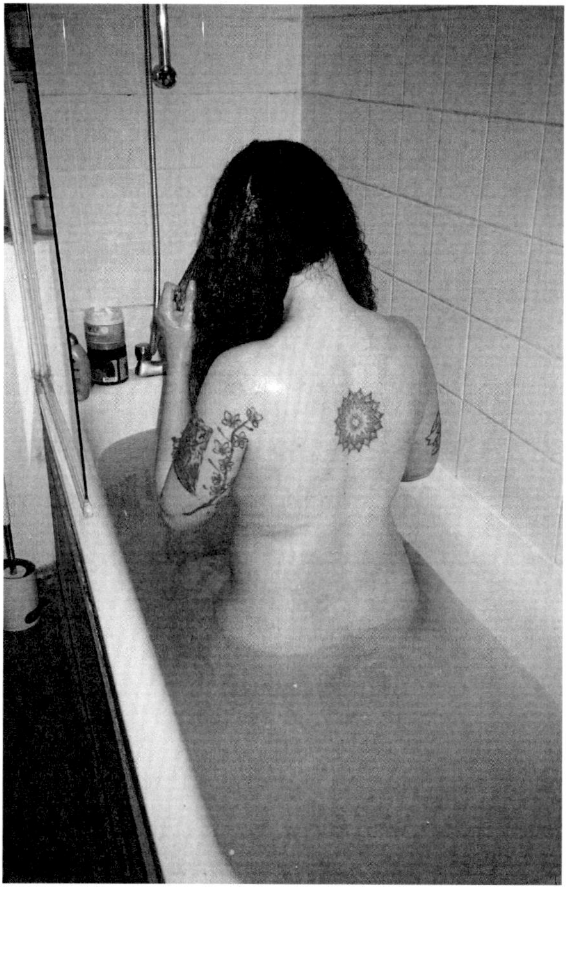

7. We've stumbled somewhere we shouldn't be, as we observe a naked person from behind, sitting in clouded bathwater. Knotted curls are coated in a congealed conditioner. Pots of toiletries are on the side of the tub. Tattoos – black line drawings – are clearly visible on the skin. On the left, a tarot card, and the branch of a cherry blossom snake up the arm. A geometric flower is right in the middle of the back. The bathroom is that of a run down, rented home, with plain features and tiles. Folds of a soft body are reminiscent of the sheets in previous images.

My nakedness is base and functional, no longer a site of pleasure, wanting, desire. I go weeks without washing. The same pair of underwear grows stagnant between my legs. My hair is a tangled web of neglect. When mum finally lifts me into the depths of a bath, the murkiness tells stories of all the places my body hasn't been, cannot go.

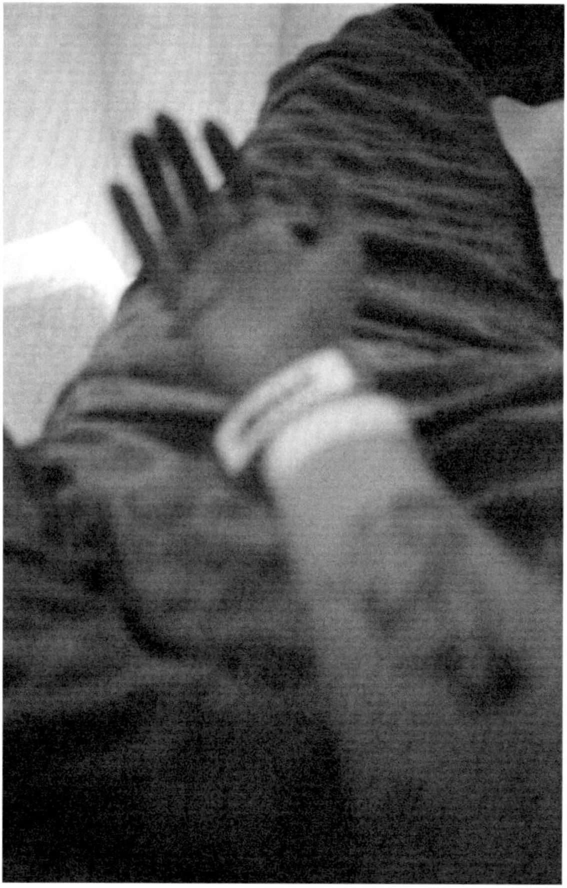

8. *I want to show you my arm. But the camera has other ideas, bringing the background into focus and leaving me ill-defined. My palm is facing upwards. Long fingers. The red hospital bracelet on my wrist reduces me to a sequence of numbers and codes. The two tattoos on my forearm are fuzzy, as if I've forgotten to put my glasses on. You can just about make out a woman. Meanwhile, the rippled blanket holds a greater clarity. A celestial glow emits from the left corner, a result of light spilling under the emerald curtain*

Projected on a monitor, I watch as tubes journey through my insides. They are detectives searching for meaning of all the ways I've gone wrong. Dark caves inhabited by half-digested food. In the haze of sedation, I think of Lizzy turning her endoscopy into art. Fictionalising her own bodily expeditions. I speak, and my words echo in the sterile room: 'this reminds me of Lizzy Rose.' The doctor looks at me, bemused, 'I treated Lizzy.' For a moment, I am not alone. A fleeting thread links me to another crip body, traversing time and mortality, flattening the divide between life and death. Unified by shared experience. I post a letter to the other side, a prayer for her safe passage, to land somewhere gentler than here, weightless, floating in space, finally free of the physical barriers that bind us.

Borough of Literature Commissions

Sauce, Sprinkles and A Flake Please Boss
Tutku Barbaros

Summer has been hiding. But we're British, so the bikini remained, tangled, on the close-to-collapsing drying rack. And the sliders waited eager on the 'welcome' mat. Just as puffer coats slumped from overuse and light denim jackets started to panic. Just as boredom truly started to grip the kids. It arrived. This wave of heat. A sigh of relief. A catalyst. An alchemy.

So now the tarmac is hot, really hot, and it's the first week of August so the air is luscious with antics. The word 'independence' bounces wall to wall. Scotch bonnet kisses baharat on the breeze to a rhythm of voice notes… low… quick… tantalisingly brief:

'weather's beautiful – what you sayin today?'

Six words and a question mark which really mean day times merging into night times, memories that will last lifetimes.

Across the 13.4 square miles of Lewisham, motives are motioned: A DJ refines remixes.

A wooden spoon is purchased for a soon-to-be fresher.

A florist arranges sunflowers,

looks at the yellow, fancies a patty and pops out for an early lunch.

The cars bend corners, windows open, bass everywhere, in me, in you, in us.

The low walls of this island of Lewisham are sat on, gathered round, congregated at.

The gentle brows of gentle boys are grazed by bucket hats

The word 'galavant' hangs on the breeze, the word 'adventure' sings through the trees.

A girl, 12, Tatlı (as in sweetness) climbs into her grandad's yellow, blue, pink (she chose the colours) ice cream van. She passes him the bright red apron he wears over his crisp white tee and they drive out of his hilltop garage and embark on a journey. Past cobbled streets only locals know of and reggae legends *everyone* knows of.

Skyscrapers glow blue in the cloudless sky.

'Did you know!?' Tatlı asks her grandad.

He loves her 'Did You Knows', claims they're from his side of the family because her mum is like that too.

'Did you know, from most of Lewisham you can see six of the ten tallest buildings in the UK?'

'I did not know.'

She always comments, 'the one called canary should be painted yellow' and he often thinks about that.

Before they've fully approached the dance school, a gaggle of girls are already twirling into queue, chased by mums worried about strawberry sauce on tutus. If Tatlı's mum was here she'd remind them that's the least of their worries, 'when raising baby girls in a brutal world.'

The girls go back to class, but the mums stay flocked outside to order screwballs (delighting in the bubblegum their daughters aren't allowed to even know about yet). The mums blow bubbles like they used to, when the dance school was on a different street, and they also shifted their feet… first position, second position, third. As they wave the ice cream van off they chirp 'Tatlı don't forget to say hello to your mum from us.'

At the sports ground a boy runs over and asks, 'what can I get for 50p?' as if he doesn't already know the answer. But there's always the joy in asking and there's always the joy in banter and sometimes, on a day like today, the ice cream man says:

'goooo onnnn have it free, but don't tell your friends, this is a business you know.'

The boy skips off happy, scores a goal like the men he roots for on the telly.

And then it's past the walrus.

Or that place that used to be a factory.

At the wishing well, where the ladies had stories to tell, a florist hopes the young man before her is buying flowers to romance a lover and not to relive a loss. She wants to ask, but language is slapped, like a rock, between them, so instead he walks around gesturing towards the ones he likes, making a globe motion with his hands and mumbling the word 'big.'

He looks at her in that way grown men sometimes do, that look where you see their boyhood shining back at you, and asks, '...good?' When it comes to flowers context is key, so our florist extends the box of cards and watches as he chooses one picturing a diamond ring surrounded by hearts, with her pen he draws a question mark. 'Good!' she confirms with newfound ease, because the flowers are gorgeous and the flowers aren't for grief. He grins a grin so big she grins too.

Triumphant, he potters out to the ice cream van and points to a sticker of what he wants. He turns back to her. Two successes, proud as a lover, growing in confidence now and calls out, 'Thank you!' 'No, thank *you*' she replies.

An over-60s walking group arrives and they order so many lemon sorbets Tatlı has to stick a 'sold out' sticker across the photo of the yellow-crowned cone. The van moves on, on, on.

Marquees are being erected outside barbershops.

And flags are waving on balconies.

Rum and raisin.

Next street.

Cherry.

Next street.

Apple lolly.

Next street.

Soft whippy.

Traffic for a moment, so the ducks can cross the road, and no one makes a sound, because Lewisham is their home too.

Next street.

Hundreds and thousands.

Next street.

The plaques telling of the men and women who made history, who changed the world, for a day, a week, forever.

Tatlı asks herself, 'What would have been their favourite flavour?'

Maybe the answer will come full circle on the South Circular.

Yes boss.

Wagwan.

Selam.

Napan beh?

Bom dia.

Geiá sou!

Afiyet olsun.

Hola.

Ciao.

Cheers!

Have a good day, mate!

As they park at the park Tatlı asks, 'Did you know there's 46 parks in Lewisham?'

She looks out at the birthday party blooming in this one, eyes bright as she watches foil trays carried in from every entrance.

A fold-out table and fold-out chairs and everyone brought a dish. A speaker is strapped to an auntie trolley. On those plastic chairs the conversations that define us for generations are taking root: a woman in her 30s natters with a cousin about a man she can't forget, a love growing, a heart ripe for breaking, but hopefully not – just as the details get juicy, Tatlı is prompted to duty.

Her mum's friends tell Tatlı about childhoods spent hearing the ice cream vans tune chug from afar, calculating if you'd make it in time, racing towards it, book bag flailing. She longs to play the music fully but she knows the rules:

A woman from somewhere called shire not sham, having recently purchased a house no one else's wages can, with two cars on her drive, counts how long the interruption lasts in the hope she can lodge a sound pollution complaint. But Tatlı only held on for 1, 2, 3 seconds. And then stopped. Not enough. The ice cream man sees the woman watching, listening, and mutters under his breath, in a mother and father tongue the woman can't comprehend, 'Hasn't she got work to do?' He wonders why, of all the things, this is what she chooses to be angry about.

For the moment, everyone's focus is on lunch rather than dessert, so Tatlı and her grandad take a breather.

Smoky sweet charcoal,

cinamon,

bubbles in plastic cups,

water balloons hurtling,

a couple kissing.

The ice cream man contemplates the young man who relied on the stickers earlier. Four decades ago the ice cream man arrived fresh, no language in his luggage, from Cyprus and has driven these streets since, learning these maps. Each road, each estate, each park sharing a type of language with all the people here, and all their different mother tongues.

Ice cream, a universal sweetness. Strawberry is pink in every dictionary. Lemon is yellow in every dialect. The blue one? A tricky to describe mystery taste which leaves its mark on every tongue and, I guess, that's why it's fun.

From the fold-out table a man calls out warmly:

'Yes, bossman! And young bosslady! You two hungry?'

'He was a boy when I came here and now he's carrying his own son,' says bossman/ice cream man/grandad to himself.

The man strides over with two paper plates:

Dollop of coleslaw.

Hill of humus.

Rice and peas.

Slice of pizza.

Two spring rolls.

Red pea stew.

Mountain of jollof.

Pasta salad.

Three dolma.

A plate licked clean is a plate licked clean in every language: delicious.

The man looks over again: 'You ready for us, yeah!?'

They all gesture a thumbs up.

As everyone is served the sun sets blue and yellow over Lewisham.

Happy birthday sung at the top of everyone's voices.

What beautiful timing:

to celebrate in an August heatwave,

to be proposed to with a bunch of flowers,

to be a 12-year-old girl in Lewisham:

summer in the palm of one hand and a chocolate vanilla oyster in the other.

208 from Lewisham Station to Orpington, Perry Hall Road

Amii Griffith

Top deck, front seat, by the window
Kids in backpacks two sizes too big
A baby cries to be heard in the din
After school chicken and chips drifts in the air
Aunties rustle blue plastic housing market stall wares
A journey through my life playing out the window pane
Sit back on the 208 the show is about to begin

Lewisham Fire Station

Transported back to 2009
Sweet smelling strawberry daiquiris
Stone cold from the slushy machine
Late nights to heavy music pulsating through my body
I lean in for a kiss
She wants to dance again
The dragon eyes my disappointment

Bromley Road / Lewisham Town Hall

Transported back to 2001
And every time since and before then
Now a hollow building hallowed
Pentecostal mouths sing praise
But not the altar I worship at
The silver screen made promises for me
And I still dream of them today

Catford Bus Garage

Transported back to 2003
Smelling burnt skin on mosquito bites
Soothed with cool aloe vera
From the land my ancestors toiled
Sav-la-Mar to Charmaine Scott
We look pretty now, yes?
Bobble band plaits straighten with a european glance

Ashgrove Road

Transported back to 2004
Or was it 2005
McDonald's breakfasts and walks down to stop DA
She would carry our drinks - hot chocolate sweet
Protect them as much as she protected me
In cold winter ice paths
Snowball fights turned violent
This world my sister's enemy

To all the places I have read
To all the places that have read me
To all the places that have raised me
The 208 – Divination of my destiny

Ode to a Bordertown
Amii Griffith

Welcome to a bordertown
Borderline personality disorientation
Disassociation
Post code switching
Don't sound like the same kitchen
Bromley graduation
To borough appreciation
Blue borough
But part of the same black and white system

Welcome to the borderland
Days spent found
Lost in woodland landscapes
More home away from home
Then I ever was now
Cold BRrrr
To South East cool
4, 6, 23
And of course the 13 ward

Welcome to the borderline
Once villains
Places I've read for me
The antihero
Of my childhood dreams
Leading the grass is greener initiative
On both sides of the fence
But only one side won
My heart in the end

Welcome to border control
Toe tipped one foot over
Blue borough Green with envy
Made to believe
We should aspire to this destiny
Welcome to my Lewisham
Where I fantasise about a knighthood
Never was a bookworm
But was a steal to make me learn

Welcome to Downham
Blue borough – Green postcode – Brown face
Educated race // To the bottom
But we come up swinging
Because some mothers do got 'em
Never bored of us
Borderless
And this is all for us

Musings
Erica Hesketh

A vibrant literary culture isn't an ornamental
shrub, but you do need somewhere to put it.

Pick a place. A hall, a library… Or a cinema,
say, in what was once a giant Poundland –

gentrification-grey poured floor, crimson sofas,
exposed vents, bookended by coffee and gin.

A place to sit for a while with a slice of cake
under strip lighting and a strange black cat.

You won't know in advance what will take.
It could be nothing… or it could be this:

the flicker of permission at an open mic
that sets in train a first collection;

a risky routine that sends laughs bursting
through a double round of heavy metal doors;

a mingling place ringed in Minion bunting,
where canons are queried and queered

and discourse flies about, all neon; and sometimes
a community choir filling the shop with song;

school kids forever shoaling in and out,
becoming whoever they want to be;

and silver screeners rapping the knuckles
of their grown-up grandchildren saying,

'You need to learn your mother tongue.'
It could be that, couldn't it? And if

you take the place away – the warm seats,
the safe spaces, the wall of tables for one

with free wi-fi for the first-time novelists –
you can bet there'll be an almighty row

but then what… what about that ornamental
shrub, that 'nice to have' which turns out

to be life-giving? It's all around us,
isn't it, rustling its multicoloured leaves,

just waiting to flourish in fresh soil?
It doesn't have to be a cinema.

It could be a dark-brick arts centre
with a community garden out the back.

Or a theatre. Or a carpark. This postcode
is resilient, we've seen it all. But we need

somewhere to gather in the dark
and let out a collective grrrowl. So please,

pick a place, keep the doors open
and let this, let *us*, grow.

Reading *A Room of One's Own* on park benches
Erica Hesketh

I line up the pram, secure the brake, lift the cover to check you're asleep, carefully drape a blanket over the top, check the bench is dry with the heel of my hand, and lower myself onto the seat. Nobody else around. Forty minutes, if I'm lucky, before you begin to mutter and stretch, like a rising loaf. I exhale, reach for my book. [

] Whenever I lose the thread of a sentence, I let my eyes wander across the grass and up to the treeline. This borough is green-veined, green-gathered, green-bursting. I love how the light dances among the willows in Sydenham Wells. The huge sky at Blythe Hill, all that space for dreaming. [

] In my memory, these minutes are always slow and balmy, though I know they can't have been. [

] One day I'm back in Ladywell Fields when a mother I've not seen since the early weeks walks by. Her mouth is an O of dismay. 'You have time to read…' I shake my head, embarrassed. But every mother should have a bench of her own, I think. [   ] For a while you won't stay asleep unless the pram is moving, so audiobooks soundtrack our slow circles round Mayow Park. There are lines of poetry from this time still scattered across the young apples. [

] Sometimes you wake after ten minutes instead of forty and we set off again. The stretch of Waterlink Way from Catford to the Bell Green Sainsbury's, flanked by patient reeds, deserves its own ode. [

] At Horniman's Triangle I fold down the page. A child clambers to the top of the rope spider-web and waves proudly to his mother, who is reading on another bench. I imagine every mother on every bench joined by a thread – all their books, their dreams, adding up to something brave, something shimmering.

                                        you know the
little tug – the sudden conglomeration of an idea at the end of one's
line

                    like a sailing-ship always voyaging never arriving, lit up
at night and visible for miles
                                                    heart, body, and
brain all mixed together

 I found myself adopting a new attitude

                              It was as if the great machine after
labouring all day had made with our help a few yards of something
very exciting and beautiful

                        imaginative work that is, is not dropped like
a pebble upon the ground

Crofton Books
Fathima Zahra

A woman   braver than me   curls spilling
out of her hat squeals
'just like my living room' – points
at books snaking up the ceiling climbing
down the rails   a chair in the midst

I put back my book   yellow
and dusting   with a love note inside (the usual).
I am looking for instructions
on how to live   and pick Ferrante
this time.

Walk down the tree-lined road
that smell of citrus in the summers
taking me back   to my aunt's house
by the river with the wind that lulls you to sleep
and she catches me   Nicholas Sparks slipping from under a textbook
I'd crept upstairs to be alone with.

No pretenses here   I inherit my room
from a writer   fill the DIY shelf
with a world beyond my passport
spines lined with plastic glint and numbers
signalling a new life.

I am pulled out of 50s Naples
by the sounds of the students next door
pulling up a mattress in the garden   stringing lights around our fence
laughter floating to the sky
like a balloon let go   just then.

On the 172 and back
Fathima Zahra

No alarm for me this morn – just the woman cussing
out her man elsewhere   not here   at the front
of the bus   I put away my book   where the writer
shuttles in and out of the hospital for her lover,
slipping away.

In the waiting room   eyes dart
between the glossy signs   and people
hunched over screens.

'I'm deffo missing an ovary'
the girl ahead of me announces
and I put my book down   probe the dark
beyond the door   where the radiographer
with a headteacher's glare summons.

In a week, the doctor will call. In fifty
pages, the woman will have slept with someone
else and the cloud breaks in the winter sky.

I walk light. Finish my book. Wink
at my past self   at the bus stop
think only of the pink roses
in our neighbour's front yard
when we first moved.

About the Contributors

Tutku Barbaros is a writer and workshop creator of Turkish Cypriot heritage, born, raised and living in Lewisham. Her debut book *All The Women She Knows – Stories Of Growth, Change & Sisterhood* was published in February 2025. *Darling Zine* called it 'the perfect women's history month read'. She's an alumna of the Royal Court Writers Programme and her debut play *LAYLA & YOUSSEF*, has been longlisted for the Bruntwood and Paines Plough Women's Prize.

Giselle Cory focuses on life writing, in particular how the small acts of life add up to our identity or come into conflict with it. They particularly enjoy work that tries to understand social history through the lens of personal experience. Recent influences include Eula Biss, Raja Shehadeh, Édouard Louis and Guadalupe Nettel. Giselle splits her time between writing and a career in the charity sector, most recently leading a small charity.

Eliezer Gore is a Zimbabwean-born artist who was raised in Lewisham. Through his art he transforms concrete reality, unveiling magical surrealist landscapes to deliver joyous affirming narratives. This year he staged an extract of his debut play, *Return to Soil*, at the Broadway Theatre in Catford for Lewisham Youth Theatre's Hatch Festival. He is the 2024 Roundhouse poetry slam runner up, Born::- Free Writers Collective alum and a Soho Theatre Writers' Lab alum.

Amii Griffith is a Lewisham-born multidisciplinary writer who has been working across stage and screen for over a decade. Amii won the Lewisham, Borough of Culture 2022 Your Words Your Lyrics Your Story spoken word competition and was recently published in *Middleground Magazine* for poets of mixed heritage. She has performed at the Actors' Church for a celebration of Noël Coward works, the

Blue Plaque unveiling of Richard Price and Catford Pride. Amii is a Soho Theatre Writers' Lab alum and Film London short film fund recipient. She recently graduated from Goldsmiths, University of London with an MA in Script Writing and is currently on the BFI-funded Trans+ on Screen script writers' development lab.

Erica Hesketh is a poet and editor, originally from Japan and Denmark, now based in Forest Hill, South East London. Widely published in magazines and journals, she placed second in the 2022 Winchester Poetry Prize, and was commended in the 2023 Magma Poetry Competition and the 2023 Stanza Competition. She was longlisted in the 2023 National Poetry Competition. From 2016 to 2024, she was Director of the Poetry Translation Centre. Her debut collection, *In the Lily Room*, will be published by Nine Arches Press in May 2025.

Oli Isaac is a writer based in London. Their passion for writing stems from growing up with a severe stutter and experiencing how language can fail us. Currently, Oli is developing their debut audio play as a recipient of Audible Theatre's Emerging Playwrights Fund. They also teach poetry workshops, most recently with The Learning Cooperative. In 2024, Oli won the Verve Poetry Festival Competition.

Jamila Prowse is an artist and writer, propelled by curiosity and a desire to understand herself. Informed by her lived experience of disability and mixed race ancestry, her work is research-driven and indebted to Black feminist and crip scholars. She is an active participant in a rich and growing contemporary disabled artistic community and has been researching, programming and creating around cripping the art world since 2018. Her writing has appeared in *Frieze*, *Art Monthly* and elsewhere

Ellie Spirrett is a poet, originally from Leeds, who started performing in Leicester and now lives in Greenwich. Ellie was a member of the Roundhouse Poetry Collective in 2023/24 and is now part of the Spread the Word Young Writers Collective. She writes about disability and ableism, chronic illness and the loneliness epidemic.

Naomi Walsh is a writer and creative based in South East London. Born and raised in Barnsley, South Yorkshire to parents hailing from Sierra Leone and Liverpool, she likes to explore identity, mixing, sonder, and (be)longing in her work. After reading English at the University of Leeds, she spent seven years working full time as a PR manager in London, earning a *PR Week* 30 Under 30 award, before going freelance in 2024 to pursue her writing.

Fathima Zahra is an Indian poet, performer and facilitator based in London. She is an alum of the Roundhouse Poetry Collective, Barbican Young Poets and BBC 1Xtra Words First. Her poems have won the Bridport Prize, Asia House Poetry Slam and Wells Fest Young Poets Prize. She has performed her work at venues across the UK including Hay Festival, Latitude and Last Word festival. Her debut pamphlet *sargam / swargam* (ignitionpress, 2021) was selected as the Poetry Book Society's pamphlet choice. She completed her MA in Creative Writing and Education at Goldsmiths, University of London, with distinction.

Thanks

This publication has been made possible thanks to the following people and organisations.

Arts Council England, the main supporters of Spread the Word and Deptford Literature Festival. Cockayne Grants for the Arts and the London Community Foundation who have supported the Emerging Writer Commissions. The Albany and Deptford Lounge, key partners for Deptford Literature Festival; and Lewisham Libraries, a key partner for the literature festival and the Lewisham Borough of Literature campaign.

Our immense thanks also to the judges and mentors who selected and supported our writers: Olumide Popoola, Joelle Taylor, Ayesha Chouglay, Joe Rizzo Naudi, Ruby Cowling, Vanessa Kisuule, Jarred McGinnis, Toby Campion, Abi Palmer and Alycia Pirmohamed.